THE BOYS WHO DANCED
WITH THE MOON

THE BOYS WHO DANCED WITH THE MOON

a novel

MARK PAUL OLEKSIW

To my Dad for always finding the time,

OVERTURE

The fabric of the night sky is often thick and heavy, capable of burying any light that tries to emerge. Many horrors fester beneath this shadowy cloak only to be exposed by the morning sun. Such was the case this warm June night—at least that was Dr. Eva Garder's fear as she parked her car on the grassy shore of a stampeding river. She knew when the sun came up that the tragedy of the night would be exposed. She wondered what awaited her in these pre-dawn hours, as she closed her car door. Her training taught her that true horror was not the sight of bloody or torn bodies. In her world, horror was measured in the number of tears in a teenage soul.

"Dr. Garder! Sorry to trouble you at this hour." Middle-of-the-night phone calls from the chief of police were as rare as they were unwelcome. Eva knew immediately from the tone of Chief Larval's voice that the situation was grave.

She looked past the broad shoulder of the chief to the activity behind him and up the hill that the led to the forest. She took in the surroundings while remaining focused on the chief. Somewhere along the way, the twenty-plus years of experience as a psychiatrist would assemble the pieces for her. "I'm here to help, as always. What happened? Did someone drown in the river? One of the local kids?"

"Unfortunately, we think so."

"You think so?"

"We haven't found a body yet. The currents are pretty strong, and who knows if we'll find anything before winter, to be honest." He looked at her dejectedly, scratching his nose with each syllable.

"What do you mean no body? Then how do you know someone drowned?"

"There were two boys that came out of that river, but from what witnesses say, three went in. When my team arrived, we found the two lying by the riverbed, one unconscious."

"Good lord, where are they?" Just then, Eva remembered an image of an ambulance speeding by her in the opposite direction on the main road leading to the hospital as she drove here. Part of her question was answered.

"One of the boys is barely alive. The paramedics did a helluva job just to get him to the hospital. We won't know for sure for a while. He was unconscious and had a shitload of water in him."

"Oh, no! What about the others? I presume that's why I'm here."

"One is very much alive, and, I suppose, doing as good as expected. He's the one who saved the kid in the ambulance, or so we think."

"Where is he? I'm guessing there's more to it." Eva could tell by the hesitation in the chief's words and his quicker-than-usual speech that he was trying to grasp the sequence of events himself.

"He's being uncooperative. He refused to tell us who he is,

so we can't even call his folks. But some boys witnessed the whole thing and called 911 from the grocery store nearby. They disappeared as soon as the paramedics and firefighters got here. They told the 911 operator three boys went into the river. The third one probably was swept away. They didn't want anyone to know who they were. The callers, I mean."

"But you know, don't you?"

"Yeah, one of my guys saw a couple of local drug dealers lurking around, watching from a distance. Advantage of our small town, it's hard to hide here."

"What are you thinking? Drugs were involved?"

"Maybe. Might be a drug deal gone bad or some kids getting high and ending up in the river."

"Chief, with all due respect, we should not jump to such conclusions." Eva's tone sharpened. Teenage issues were not always drug-related, nor were teenagers always up to no good.

"Sure, but I get paid the big bucks to jump to those conclusions." Just as Chief Larval finished his statement, a plainclothes policeman came running up behind him.

"Chief, excuse me, we found something you need to see in some shrubs near where we think these boys went in."

"A body?"

"No, sir. We found this old haversack. We didn't open it. We figured you'd want to see it first."

The chief eagerly ripped the bag out of the hands of the younger subordinate. "Thanks. I know what we'll find in here." A broad smile raced across his face while he fumbled for the opening of the bag. He brought the open bag to his face with his chin almost leaping forward. After a second or two, his smile retreated, and his left hand dove inside, feeling around the bag. His face became blank and expressionless.

"Hmm, Chief, seems you found what you may not have been looking for." Eva tried not to let sarcasm seep into her voice. Out of the corner of her eye, she saw the young plainclothesman wink at her. Crap, she thought. He heard it.

"Here. This situation may be up your alley." Chief Larval handed her the bag while rolling his eyes.

She took the haversack and gently opened it wide enough to see its contents. She raised her eyebrows quickly as she reached in and with great care pulled out a large notebook filled with page after page of loose paper trapped between the bound pages. She opened up the notebook and came upon a folded page at the front. Carefully unfurling the page, she read it, her eyes widening with each word. She quickly refolded the paper and tucked it back in before delicately placing the notebook back inside its keeper.

"I need to see the boy right away." She handed the bag back to the chief. "Take good care of this—someone will want it back."

"I honestly thought we would find drugs in there."

"No, Chief. This is not about drugs or alcohol."

Chief Larval shook his head dismissively. He knew better than to challenge her, though. "I'll take care of it. The boy you'll find over there." He pointed about one hundred yards away to a clearing near the riverbank.

Emboldened by the task at hand, Eva made her way to the figure sitting alone. Her eyes studied him while she committed to memory any movement or gesture made by the teenager as she approached. There was minimal activity to observe. The boy had a maroon-colored blanket wrapped around his shoulders. He sat on the grass with his knees bent and his legs spread apart. His eyes stared into the distance. Were they hypnotized by the moon, water, or trees along the riverbank? It was impossible to tell. Even when she was within a few feet of him, he didn't budge, not even to acknowledge her entering his space. She paused and stood a few feet from him, her eyes intensely focused, like a student studying minutes before a final exam.

She could see his face trembling and lips quivering. The river odor settled under her nose. Droplets of water occasionally trickled down his cheek. His brown hair, almost the color of night, remained wet and matted. His shoulders were broad and the blanket barely covered him. He wore a curious-looking jacket, faded blue jeans, and a cross around his neck. Even from his profile, she could see the blank stare, looking at everything but finding nothing. In her world, this was pure horror. No blood, no severed limbs; everything missing and nothing left. She pursed her lips to stifle a sigh. The task ahead would be daunting. It was not often that she couldn't find the right words, but this was one of those times. The boy then shivered slightly and his first movements were to adjust the blanket on his back, pulling it tighter against his body.

A maxim that came less from formal training and more from her fundamental beliefs formed the words that tumbled out of her mouth. "The moonlight accents the beauty of the flowing water. It reminds me of how timeless this planet is. The water searching for an even bigger body to merge…" she paused, waiting for the words to be fully absorbed. "I can't imagine how you must feel. Sitting here with an infinite sky above you and a lonely river at your feet, only to be here by yourself, with a blanket not large enough to keep you warm, and a friend in an ambulance and another in the river." She waited again, this time extending the seconds between words. "Yes, with a bigger blanket you would be at least warm. You deserve better for saving your friend." Her hands slid around her waist, and her fingers entangled themselves behind her in hope.

The words drifted out of the young man's mouth as a ballet dancer flutters across a room. He didn't move or twitch as he spoke. His eyes remaining fixed and searching directly ahead.

"All he wanted was to dance. You know. He kept hearing this music and thought it sucked for no one to be dancing to it."

Eva smiled meekly. "Your friend, he liked to dance? He wanted to dance?"

In a voice lacking any hint of emotion, he replied, "It was under a moon, like tonight, that he got us to dance with him." There was a discernible sigh. "We didn't dance very long or very well."

Eva moved closer and crouched down until she was next to him, staring out at the stars, in the same manner as he. "Your friend, the dancer, is he the one they took to the hospital?"

"Well, not really. Not better than me anyways. The dancer

is gone. We tried to save him. My friend did his best to save him."

"I'm sure you did, too. These waters are very dangerous this time of year."

"Will he survive, my friend who they took? I need to know. He tried so hard in the water. He almost gave his life and would have, too. I had to pull him up with all my might." He turned now to face her. His eyes, bleary and tired, glared at her intensely.

"The doctors and nurses will do everything in their power to make sure he survives. Equally important, how are you? I imagine your parents are worried."

"I don't think you understand. My friend has to make it. He has to."

"Why don't you tell me what happened tonight? How you saved your friend from the river—I am sure that's quite a story. Maybe you'll tell me after we call your parents."

The boy grew silent. His fingers slid along the grass, pulling out blades and squeezing them in his hands. "I'm not good at telling stories, at least ones with any truth to them." He chuckled ever so slightly. "He's the storyteller. Yes, he can put the words around it for you to understand what happened tonight. I could never do it."

"I'm sure you can tell me in your words. I have no doubt you could." She leaned over and gently placed her hand on his shoulder.

The boy sprang up quickly and took two strides toward the river before stopping and turning back to her. "I will make a promise to you. If you can make a promise to me."

"I'm not too good with promises. I do have a Ph.D. in listening."

"Well, if you save him, he'll tell you the story. He's the only person I want telling the story of what happened. You have to save him, though. My friend has to live."

"If he tells me the story, is he the type who likes his stories with happy endings? Is that why he should tell it?"

He threw his head back and seemed to search the sky. His hands dug into his front pockets, and he shrugged. "Yesterday that answer was clear. Tonight and tomorrow, I don't think so. What I do know for sure, more surely than anything in my heart, is that I would give anything to hear him tell that story."

Eva smiled at him. "I'm sure the story will include dancing, too."

"My friend would reach for the moon. Shit, I believed he could. The night sky is just charcoal, and if you reach too high, it smears your hands, your lungs, and everything until all you are is stained."

The blanket slipped off his shoulder, but he seemed to pay it no mind as he said, "Or even dead."

PART 1: A SILENT MOON
CHAPTER 1
My Hometown, June 2006

When I opened my eyes, pure terror took over. I searched my memory for a picture or image resembling my current surroundings and came up empty. I was on a soft brown fabric couch in what appeared to be an old, dingy living room. There was a hint of cigar smoke from years past seeking escape from the furniture. The banisters and moldings consisted of burgundy-colored oak last stained decades ago. The floors were hardwood and bore the signs of thousands of footsteps. The smell of sweet but subtle perfume—the scent of a freshly peeled apple— briefly put my mind at ease and was the only touch of the present in the air.

My shoes were neatly placed near the couch. Thankfully, I was fully clothed. My mind was overrun with clouds, my thoughts gasping for air and troubling me to no end. I studied my clothes and determined I was wearing what I had on when I left my starkly furnished apartment the previous evening. But where was I—and how did I get here? What happened?

I sat upright on the edge of the couch and cupped my hands to support my head. I could feel the tears welling up in my eyes, pumped by my fear. Memory loss and lost time were not strangers to me. This wasn't the first time that I couldn't recall what happened to me, but the feeling of not having any control of myself still frightened me. I was startled when a feminine voice bellowed from behind me, almost from another world.

"How are you doing this morning?" A long silence followed before the voice continued. No doubt my bewilderment was evident to her. "Do you remember what happened? I brought you here. You don't need to be scared," she said in a steady but tender voice.

For some reason, I did feel reassured. It was a fresh voice to me. I slowly turned to see who brought me here. The young woman could not have been more than five foot three or four with wavy, reddish hair and green, sparkling eyes. She looked like she was in her early twenties. There was something odd about her—I felt a familiarity that I couldn't pinpoint to any place or moment. Obviously, my being in her house without a plausible explanation was bizarre.

"Sorry. I'm really confused. Who are you, and how did I get here? I guess I blacked out?" My tone was blunt, and I regretted it immediately.

"Well, you do have a curious way about getting a girl to take you back to her place. I can tell you that much."

I took her comment quite seriously. Not wanting her to think I orchestrated something I didn't, I quickly shook my head. "Honestly, this isn't some come on. I mean, I'm quite a bit older than you and . . ." She was attractive in a curious, though awkward, way. Her eyes seemed to change color as she spoke. I couldn't look into them because I felt like if I did, they'd devour me whole.

She rolled her eyes. "Yes. I can tell you're getting on in years . . ." My fear must've been obvious because her playfulness came to a halt as if on cue. "You got sick last night and passed out at the pub. You were lucky I happened to be there. The manager threatened to call the police."

"Shit! I didn't drink anything potent at all. Did I? How did it happen?"

"You weren't drinking anything stronger than an iced tea, but you just fell over. They checked you for identification. I was sitting nearby so I told them I knew you and would get you home. A couple of other customers helped you into my car. The California driver's license threw the manager off a bit. You're quite a way off the grid."

"You didn't have to go to all that trouble. Look, let me know how I can repay you and I'll get out of your hair."

"No worries at all. You seemed like a nice enough guy." She crouched down and studied me carefully. A tight smile stretching across her lips.

Uncomfortable under the scrutiny, I looked around for some exit.

"Sorry, I'm a psych major at the university. I like to observe. Maybe I take my training too seriously. I know it's a little unnerving. Half the time I don't even realize I'm doing it."

"No problem. I get a lot of people trying to understand me. Hell, not even *I* understand me sometimes." Realizing I said way too much, I pulled myself up off the couch and as I did, two surprisingly strong arms pushed me back down. This stranger seemed to know how to probe and the art of gentle interrogation was one skill she appeared to have mastered.

"Slow down! People do not black out like you did for no reason. Like I said, you barely drank anything. At least come to the kitchen and have breakfast with me."

"You've done too much already . . ."

"I don't think you get it. You have two choices. Either at least settle in for breakfast so I know you're fine, or I'm calling an ambulance for you right now."

My natural inclination was to flee. Embarrassed by my weaknesses and in the house of stranger, running was the logical option. Yet when I looked at her, I recognized something in her smile and eyes that calmed me. It would be days before I understood why. "Easy choice," I declared sheepishly.

She walked away, giving me an opportunity to study her. I noticed she dressed very conservatively. She wore a red sweater and black jeans with a barely noticeable amount of makeup. There was an undeniable mystery surrounding her. I did remember going to the pub, and I recalled a redhead sitting nearby. Trying with complete focus, I visualized getting into a car, but that's where the memory ended.

As I got up to walk to the kitchen table, I glanced around the room. It featured relatively few modern surroundings interspersed with more antique features, including quite a few books on a shelf. In the corner of the room was a small desk with a computer. It was the kind of place you would expect from a student, which eased my cynical mind. I had enough on my plate, both literally and figuratively, without fearing this woman.

The smell of eggs, bacon, and coffee was a welcomed treat.

It seemed like ages since I'd had a hearty breakfast and I was famished. Back in California, Avery was a decent cook, but by the time I got anything, reheating was often required. Rob and Avery's leftovers were nevertheless appreciated, if sparse. I sat down at the kitchen table, the stranger across from me with a grapefruit on her plate. She noticed my eyes shifting as I grew fascinated as to why she was eating something different and far healthier.

"I don't really eat breakfast. I just guessed it was what you would like. I suppose I was right," she said with her eyebrows raised as I finally lifted my gaze up from my dish. The breakfast was beyond appetizing.

"This is all a little . . . you know."

"Weird." She started laughing loudly. "I'm not sure who's more scared of who." She saw my hands clench and quickly slid the toast closer to me, like a peace offering.

"Have you blacked out before? You don't look well. You seem like you've lived a million lifetimes. Or maybe none at all. California is quite a way from our fair town. Must be some story to your trek here." Her focus turned away from me, and it seemed like she was proud of her observation.

I tried to think of all my options as I pondered her question. There was no way she was going to let me off the hook. How could I keep her from getting involved? She didn't need to deal with my problems. She was a psych major and far too inquisitive. But there was no reason to doubt her intentions at this point. It was pointless not to answer her question at least since she did do me a great favor and saved me from a trip to the hospital.

"I have blacked out before. A little less than a month ago was the last time."

"Wow. Were you checked out by a doctor?"

"I had a CT scan, X-rays, blood tests. You name it; they probed it. They found nothing wrong." I hadn't actually gone through all of those tests, but told a similar lie to appease Avery at the time. My problems were far from being physically detectable.

"No, not a medical doctor. I mean a psychologist."

"Geez, you truly do not mince words. No, but I am pretty sure there're more people than you can imagine who would enjoy seeing me in a straitjacket." Remembering the look upon Mr. McCastle's face when I walked out of his office weeks ago, I laughed at my joke.

"Not to be rude, but if you have some issue, maybe I can refer you to someone. I know I'm just a student, but I might know the right person. I even know some hypnotists. Some of the ones I know achieve impressive progress with the right patient."

"What you did for me last night was more than enough and, to be truthful, I really shouldn't intrude any longer. I'll be all right." I nibbled on a piece of toast and quickly got up to put my plate in her dishwasher before making my way to the closest door.

She seemed startled by my actions before jumping up and intercepting me before I reached the door. There were two doors. It was the story of my life. I wasn't sure which one to open and took my cue from her eyes. Unfortunately, the door was locked and, in my haste, I couldn't navigate the lock. She seized upon the opportunity to block my exit.

"Not every day that a lady makes a breakfast like that for a man she just met. The least you can do is show some gentlemanly courtesy and allow me to indulge in my need to be a Good Samaritan."

"Do you know what I was doing before I blacked out?"

"No, umm . . . not really. The pub had the local news on the overhead television. There was a newspaper on your table when you toppled over. Luckily, you didn't hit your head." She was suddenly hesitant in the details, but I chose to let it go.

I glanced back at her and made the mistake of catching her eyes. I had seen the Medusa and froze from taking further action. "I just don't want to bother you. You're a smart person with a bright future from what I gather. You don't need my problems."

She sighed as she unlocked the door. "Sorry for being a bit selfish. Helping is very self-actualizing for me. I know I can handle anything. You cannot even imagine what I'm capable of," she said with a fiery tone contrasting her delicate voice.

I walked through the doorway and she grabbed the door just as I was about to shut it. "If you change your mind and need someone to talk to, you're more than welcome to come back. My name is Rachel. Maybe you'll even tell me what brings you to our quaint town." She grinned at me.

"Well, maybe. For now, thanks for everything. I'm Kiran Wells," I said as I closed the door. Of course, she must have known that already, having seen my driver's license.

When the door shut behind me, the solitary nature of my

return to my hometown overwhelmed me and felt ominous. What I was unprepared for, as I ventured outside beneath the heat of the morning light, was how my past patiently waited just outside the reach of Rachel's house.

CHAPTER 2

I stumbled onto the street, my eyes adjusting to the brightness of the morning. To my consternation, everything around me became evocatively familiar. I looked back at Rachel's home, hoping to make some sense out of everything that had happened. It looked just as old on the outside as it did on the inside. The shingles on the roof appeared ready for take off with the most modest gust of wind. The lawn in front apparently had not been pampered with any landscaping.

I couldn't deny that I had a blackout episode at the pub. Miraculously, it had never happened in a public place before. My prolonged slumber years ago was likely the cause. Given that I had been under a lot of self-inflicted stress and anxiety, the great surprise was that it didn't occur more frequently. The circumstances of the night before remained ambiguous, and how it had played out troubled me. I reasoned I was fortunate that this strange and simultaneously approachable student had rescued me.

The more I thought of her, the more I realized circumstances demanded further scrutiny. A lovely girl taking in this old, broken soul sounded like the plot of a lighthearted movie. I debated going back inside to find out more about my friendly young patron. My conclusion was her hospitality earned her a free pass from my troubles. I rubbed my face, knowing full well the heaviness of my plight. My hands ran through the thick coat of hair covering my sensitive skin, the by-product of having not shaved since landing. Aside from passing out the night before, I had not slept very much or very well either.

There was a ghost-town vibe emanating from my surroundings. Suddenly, I could hear a gentle roar in the distance, a sound diabolically frightening for a reason I dared not try to understand. Flowing water was nearby! I had been so involved with my thoughts about the house I just left that I failed to notice where I was. The water was most surely the Pauley River.

My heart pounded even before I ran down the street to get a better view of the source of the noise. Once I caught a line of vision, I felt like I was being hit by a rapid succession of lightning bolts. I took a knee to the ground as I fought with every inch of my fiber from blacking out again. I realized Rachel might be watching from her window and would not hesitate to rescue me a second time. My shoelaces were quickly untied and then retied to suggest I bent down with a trivial purpose.

I knew once I had seen the river, Shep's Hill would be visible soon enough. This area was most definitely near my old stomping grounds, which I'd been avoiding since coming back. That much I recollected beyond any doubt. Without a car and on foot, there was no way I was anywhere close to this region last night. Now here, I thought back to my trip to Pauley River a couple of weeks ago.

I had tried to sleep on the five-hour flight, but my thoughts raced faster than the pacing I did from the front to the back of the plane. It was only the turbulence that got me to sit. The flight attendant kept asking if I needed assistance, and I blamed it on a fear of flying, even though I had flown hundreds of times.

I hadn't been back to Pauley since I left twenty years ago. My parents moved soon after my departure. They, too, fled to the warmer pastures of the south. The presumption was the demons chasing me would somehow search for them as well, and they would be easy targets if they stayed behind.

Pauley was a small town outside of a growing metropolitan city. You grew up in Pauley and eventually, if everything went well, went off to the local college, Riverside. Those with money could afford the more expensive schools of the south. The majority stayed and continued their education here. Many found jobs in the big city miles away, returning home each evening to the quiet suburban life. Living in Pauley was generally a cradle to grave existence. Not that it was a bad place to grow up. Nor a horrible place to die.

The town had one high school occupying a central location at the base of Shep's Hill. Years ago, some town elder tried to get Shep's Hill renamed Mount Shep. It was a hill; no more, no less. On the opposite side of Shep's Hill was the Pauley River. Once you climbed the hill, you reached a forest that hid the path to the river on the other side of its steep slope. Swimming was not permitted, since the currents could get unyielding at certain times of the year. The Pauley River snaked through the outskirts of our town, marking the separation between the here and anyplace else.

On top of Shep's Hill was a chalet for those using the ice rink that went up in the winter and came down in the spring. Within the bowels of the forest was an old rundown shack that most people avoided, claiming it housed a crazy hermit who haunted the town a hundred years ago. The shack was a favorite hiding spot for the local teens who needed a quiet place to go where their parents wouldn't find them. The shack, made of plain pine planks, was cold and uninsulated during the winter season, and hot and dingy during the summer. It was a convenient place to go from time to time to be alone with your thoughts. It would be a source of refuge for me, and a memory painted over through the years.

Pauley High had about six hundred students back then. Girls and boys were pretty much split evenly in number. The school was refurbished in the early 80s, but by the time I went to it, the signs of age were already showing again. On the other side of the river was the larger college, which had ten thousand students. It was a more modern building and attracted students from Pauley and other neighboring towns.

My father and mother had both followed ritual by going to the high school and the local college. I always assumed I would slog down that same academic path. Along that trail, I would either be dragging friends with me or riding their coattails.

When I fled, I left behind miniscule traces of my existence, like a squirrel's tracks before a snowstorm. The intent was that nobody would hunt me down or find me. My parents had made sure of it. They wanted my future to be safe from my past. Conveniently, I forgot about the reason I needed to leave. Conveniently, I couldn't remember the night of my accident.

It was an escape and an illusion worthy of comparison with the finest of Houdini's performances. It was not yet the middle of June when I headed back east. When the plane landed, I could see the sun beginning to set in the west from whence I had come. I never expected to return.

I could only imagine Rob's reaction when he heard what I had done. Rob was tough and a consummate game player. He would one day forgive me. He had no choice. Avery would never let him hold a grudge against me.

As I stepped off the plane, the world around me seemed trapped in a web, waiting for a hungry spider to return and nibble on whatever it caught. The sense of purpose I had when I left Beckett and Bells had waned, and the uncertainty of what was to come paralyzed me temporarily upon my return. I could hear ancient watches unwinding with a grinding sound. Sadly, there was no welcoming band for this homecoming. Time would be a competitive foe.

Then, as if on cue, Rachel had brought me here of all places, which meant she had been out last night in a pub that was a sizable distance from her home. The coincidence was too extraordinary. Who was she?

Rachel could not have been more than twenty or so, that much was certain. I was likely long gone from here before she was even a toddler. The present was awash with coincidences and voices from the past whispering sugary haunted nothings. So much more was eating away at me from the inside. I knew I would have to come to this area one day. I just didn't think it would be today.

I looked back at the house that was now a block away and took a mental note of the address. If she wanted to harm me or rob me, it would have already happened. While the thought of her taking a romantic interest in me was appealing, I was a realist enough to know otherwise. Ghouls with beards don't do well in romances though. I was no werewolf.

I found a bus route and got general directions on how to get back to where I was staying. My landlady must be freaking that I had disappeared for so long. My thoughts swam while paranoia circled me like a starving shark. I went to the back of the bus. While I had enough money for a cab, I needed time to think. Hopefully, the bus ride would jar memories free. No way could I stomach a conversation with a curious cab driver.

Why had I returned? On the surface, it was because of the letters. What was I trying to accomplish here? I stayed so far away from where I was raised and then when I finally ended up in my old neighborhood, I was running away again. Where to begin untangling all these knots? Intuitively, I knew I could find someone from the old days if I tried. I could easily go back to my old neighborhood. The sense of great peril trapped and enslaved any courage I could muster. I would be confronting emotions returning from a black hole, light years away. I felt a cold shiver. I had gone far enough on this one journey today and had enough to ponder.

When the bus brought me to the opposite end of town and farther away from the sound of the river, I finally started to breathe more easily.

Walking from the bus stop to my apartment, I could see my landlady hiding behind the gray curtains of her foyer, watching me. It would be moments before she was out on the front steps. I slowed my steps to face the inevitable, and sure enough, her door opened just as I was putting my key into the lock.

"Oh, hello!" My tone was far too excited.

"Everything okay?" She didn't let me answer. "I had some leftover lasagna and was going to give it to you. Your loss since you didn't return last night."

"Sorry. I took your advice, went to the bistro, and after the bistro met a couple of old friends and . . ."

"Friends? Really. You were gone all . . ." Suddenly, there was a twinkle in her eye. "Yes, friends. I remember when I was young." She smirked and my face turned the color of a ripe beet. "Wait a second." She ran back into the house and came back with a plate. "You look hungry. Take it. You can warm it up later."

"Thanks, and please don't worry about me."

"I came to bring you lasagna and a message. Someone was trying to call you yesterday. I heard the phone ring a few times last night from your place. I've barely heard it ring since you arrived—it was strange."

"It was probably one of my friends from back home." Probably Avery or Rob since no one knew my number here. I brought no smartphone with me either.

Upon thanking her again for the food, I climbed the stairs to my rental. I could see a spider had started its web on the inside of the windowpane. I ignored it. I was exhausted and wanted to nap. I was too tired to undress and just laid back on the couch as I slid into cavernous thought.

Trying with the best of intentions, I visualized myself leaving my current abode last night to find a place to eat. I ran into the landlady on my way out, and she recommended a place called Jack's Bistro and Burgers. It was a pub-type place—a fancy hamburger joint—that served imported beer. I remembered the waitress getting my order. She asked if I wanted a beer and I could hear my voice say "no." Through the haze of my memory, I tried to picture some of the people sitting in the restaurant near me. Eating by yourself in a small town will usually draw some interest. I did recall some of the other patrons. I most certainly did ask the waitress for a newspaper. Yes, that's what I did, and that was all I could recollect.

I must have drifted off to sleep because two hours later I awoke to the sound of the phone ringing. It was an anxious ring. I could tell.

"Hello."

"Kiran! Is everything all right? I've been trying to reach you since yesterday." It was Avery, sounding frantic, nearly hysterical.

"I'm fine, Avery. Fine. How are you and Rob?"

"Fine? Where were you yesterday? We were ready to fly out! Especially after the girl called and we didn't hear from you. I felt so guilty for not stopping you."

"Girl called? The girl called who? You?"

"Yes. Yes. Someone called here looking for you the other

day. I told her you weren't home."

"This person called you?"

"No. Your place. I was there watering your plants and the phone rang. I thought it might be your dad."

"Hmm. So what did this girl say?"

"She sounded sweet and young. She said she was a relative of yours and needed to reach you."

No one had tried to contact me in years from either my mom's or dad's side of the family.

"What else did she say?"

"I told her that you'd gone back to your hometown. She said she was living there now, and that's why she wanted to get in touch with you."

"That is interesting." I could tell Avery was getting concerned, mainly sensing that I seemed confused. I knew what I had to do. "What did you say to her?"

"Well, she sounded sincere, so I gave her your number and told her where you were staying. The more I thought about it, the more I realized I made a mistake giving her your coordinates. Did she find you? We tried calling, and nobody answered, so we got worried. Damn you for not taking your phone with you!"

"Avery, don't be a mother hen. She never called here. I went out last night to get a bite and was watching the ball game at a place near here. When I got back, it was kind of late. I didn't want to wake you."

"It's three hours earlier here, Kiran."

"Oops. Yeah, right. Forgot. I guess I was so tired that I probably crashed and didn't hear the phone."

"Are you sure? She never contacted you?"

"No. I must have missed her call, too. I'll let you know if she calls again."

"If you need help, call us."

"Yeah, no problem. You say she sounded youngish?" I asked hesitantly.

"Yes, why?"

"Nothing. You know, it's rare for a young lady to be calling for me nowadays, right?" I tried to add some levity.

"Ha, ha! Maybe you need some young woman in your life!"

"Thanks, Mom, and stop worrying," I said hanging up the phone. I avoided asking her about Rob. I didn't need to deal with his anger.

I stared at the spider finishing the last loop on his silky prison cell. Whoever called my place knew my address and was probably the one who sent me the letters. I rushed out of my apartment quickly, ran down the stairs, and rang the bell of my landlady. She opened the door cautiously. I'd never rung her doorbell before.

"Everything okay?"

"Just a question. Did you see a red-haired girl around here yesterday?" The moment I said it, I laughed somewhere deep inside at the Charlie Brown–esque nature of my question.

"Now, Mr. Wells, don't play games with me. Of course, I did. She did catch up with you and your friends?"

I played along and nodded my head. "So you spoke to her."

"Of course, she rang my bell looking for you. I told her you would be at the bistro. She *did* catch up to you, right?" She had a soft twinkle in her eye.

"Right. Umm . . . she just never told me how she found me."

"I take it she found you. You were with friends, as you say." She was now laughing at her humor and slowly closed the door.

My god! It had to be Rachel who called Avery. She'd gone to the extent of stalking me. *Why*? The realization felt like nuclear fallout to my already fragile state. My heart raced with fear, and horror coursed through my veins. It could only have been Rachel. It was too coincidental. It was too far-fetched otherwise. That night, I awoke curled up into a ball. I had the covers wrapped tightly around me, holding on for dear life. I had left the window open to get some fresh air, and it helped me doze off. Now it sent a chill through me. The spider was gone, leaving behind the web. I carefully closed the window, not wanting to damage the product of its toil.

Filled with nervous energy, I got up and made instant coffee and pulled out the remaining leftovers from the previous evening. I sat at my kitchen table and picked at the now cold lasagna. Damn, it always tasted so good cold. Lasagna and pizza. Best leftover dishes of all time. I tried to talk myself out of what I was planning to do next. No matter what, I always came back to the same conclusion.

Rachel must have waited outside my building when I left for supper. Had she wanted to harm me, she had plenty of opportunities. Even if she was in such dire need to see me, she had still kept her distance. She was observing me. Why? I wondered. She was way too young to own a piece of the puzzle rattling around somewhere in my head. The first letter I understood. It wasn't hard to get an old newspaper clipping. But the second letter—it was impossible for her to have what she sent me, or so I thought.

My heart told me she was a kind person. No doubt she was almost obsessive about helping me. I finally concluded I had to take the chance. Hell, if she did indeed write me and called me back home, I needed to see her or else I would be spinning my wheels wandering around on this side of town for years.

It was almost exactly twenty years ago. I thought I'd escaped the river long ago and found the illusion of peace by the ocean when I'd left this place. But time was knocking on my door, and its patience was wearing thin.

CHAPTER 3
California, May 2006

Water was too seductive for me to ignore for too long in my life. I'd left the river and gone straight to the ocean. When I first came out west to the Golden State and started my career with an investment banking firm fresh out of school, I sought long and hard to find a place by the beach. Desperate was my attempt to escape the cold from the east where my youth took shape. I searched for a spot close enough to the center of the city where I would work and be at a minimum walking distance to the coast. I settled into an apartment in a purely physical sense. My mind, however, was like fog hovering over a river in the early morning, drifting wherever the wind would take it and often traveling far from where it originated.

Sporadic friendships entered my life while I tried to become a part of the community. In reality, I was part of the community in the same way a statue becomes part of the church within which it stands guard. Within a crowd there always is a token loner, maybe two. It was always a safe bet I was one of them.

I would go to various parties and disappear into the blinds. A professional chameleon was I, doing party tricks for those who cared to observe. Nobody did. I would sit and take everything in while going undetected. I perpetually observed people and their interactions as a way to wind my clock forward.

What kept me sane or insane, however one wants to interpret it, was relative. I stayed away from business books, although my bosses and mentors pushed them on me like cheap narcotics. Reading about the universe and a lot about history kept my mind busy. No networking, no social media, no outside world beyond my necessary existence. I doubt Plato's cave was as desolate a place. Shadows were my fear, so I kept the sun out.

I worked my way up and took on many challenges, often traveling to remote and distant places. I never put myself up for promotion, as I didn't want any additional responsibility. A comfortable living is what I earned and, more importantly, I had my fortress of solitude close to the beach. Those who approved my paycheck appreciated the single workaholic who was consistently prepared to run to the next assignment. They thought I was running *to* something. That was the genius of my game. In the mirror of my existence, what was "running to" was actually "running from." My "mentors" gave up trying to forge false friendships with me as they, too, worried about how deep into my web they could get caught if they were not careful.

There was one trick I had learned since leaving my hometown. Stay busy. Keep moving. Never let the past catch you standing still. The past was always chasing me and searching for me. What I had been too foolish to understand was that years ago, it embedded itself within me.

The Pacific Ocean was my mistress. It taunted me at night with its stars dancing in the sky. The waves would sing to me with their roar vibrating in my ears. I tried to learn to surf but never quite mastered it. I would often go to the beach late at night when it was quiet and sit and read in the moonlight. The waves and seeming infinity of the ocean seemed to call to me. I would wander out into the darker and deeper waters to see how far I would go or—better yet—dare to go. When I felt the waves daring me to go a little farther, something inside me, besides the frigid waters, would hold me back. Partly fear, partly something much deeper. There was an incompleteness in my heart that would not fill so quickly with saltwater. Time passed between my toes in the form of beige and endless coarse sand.

Girls and pseudo-girlfriends came and went from time to time. Most were fascinated with my title and my position. However, a coat of fresh paint can only hide the fact the house required condemnation for so long. Eventually, the exterior becomes weathered and the rotting wood, visible. Nobody can tolerate a haunted loner for too long.

The term "haunted" came up a lot. The wise ones would see it in my eyes. The dark coals did not sparkle when they searched for their reflection within them, scaring even the bravest. Instead, they saw a barren black corridor where no memories dared roam. I had chosen to stay on this Ferris wheel and ride the coattails of time as it lurched forward.

I felt like a glass far too deep to be filled by anything, though my greatest fear was being perpetually empty. Eventually, I drilled far down enough to the core of my feelings to know the vibrations within me only proved I was hollow.

One summer night, I ventured way out into the ocean, the waves pushing me out even farther. The calling and pull were strong. My loneliness sapped the strength from my feet, and I almost got caught. Garnering enough energy to fight off the waves, I headed back to shore, tired though alive. It was with profound sadness that I waded out of the water. I despised my work. Always did. The weight of that burden had grown on me, and it was a matter of time before I surrendered to the charm of the waters. The inevitability of the outcome was never in doubt.

My father never saw the same magic in the waters that I did or maybe it was the hypnotic effect over me that worried him. My parents had long since retired, and their health had degenerated just when they could enjoy life. Around the time of my thirtieth birthday, I had spent countless weekends traveling back and forth to visit them. Within hours of landing and arriving back to my place one night, my father called with the news; my mom had succumbed to cancer.

I offered my home to my dad immediately, since I had plenty of space. He refused to be a martyr so he chose a retirement community in the south. I would visit him every few months. While physically weaker each time, his mind grew finer and sharper. Again, I would ask him if he wanted to stay with me. He would always refuse. The last time he visited, he walked with me along the beach the night before he headed back.

He stopped suddenly and lowered his round black glasses and smiled while placing his hands on my shoulders. My father was not a man of many emotions or words. The seriousness of his tone struck me before the words even came out.

"Your mother and I always tried to do the best thing for you. You know that? Yes?"

"I've always known that."

"We have not always been right. We tried to protect you."

"Um . . ." I tried to pretend I didn't know it was forgiveness he sought. So many emotions arose like molten lava awakening within a mountain. "Please, Dad. The past is the past. Things have worked out for the better," I said sternly yet calmly. This road he was preparing to travel on was treacherous, for me especially. My dad needed to see me strong before he returned home. It was the only forgiveness I could offer him. I needed to lie bravely.

He looked up at the stars and back to me. "Promise me one thing."

"What? Anything, Dad. You know that."

"Be happy. Whatever it takes, you must not stop until you find it."

I didn't argue because I could see the moment of epiphany flash in his eyes. Not knowing what to say fueled my silence. Pretending again not to know what he was referring to, I didn't pursue a further explanation.

Observing our footprints in the sand as I looked back, I noticed mine now larger than his, sadly, though, they swayed from side to side, aimless.

We didn't talk much more that night. It was the last time he came to visit me in California. It must have pained him too much to see me there alone and miserable, however brave a face I sloppily painted on for him to study.

CHAPTER 4

I walked along the beach one night a few weeks later. I remembered in vivid detail the last conversation between my dad and me. Replaying his message over in mind, as if it would somehow change with every playback, I wasn't paying attention. Clumsily, I stumbled upon someone lying in the sand right where the water met the shore. I landed nose-first into the packed wet grit.

"So sorry," I said to this poor woman. My face was caked lightly in the sand, and some of it nestled itself in my eyes and hair. As I brushed it out, I heard a gentle voice reply.

"No. Don't be. I'm okay," said the youthful stranger. "I must have dozed off."

A tattered light blue blanket sprawled across her bony shoulders. She wore cut-off jeans and a red T-shirt. Her hair was tied with a pink ribbon at the back. She had bottomless, bright green eyes and wavy hair that seemed oily and appeared almost mustard colored. She had a slightly emaciated frame and looked as though she hadn't showered in a while. She was just out of her late teens. There she was, alone, lying on the beach well past midnight, but her eyes displayed no signs of fear.

It would have been easy for me to move on. I couldn't. I told her how I lived nearby and had for years. Never had I met anyone who stared as intently at me as she did. Examining my face and my eyes with her own as if skilled at sizing up people in an instant, I stood before her, entranced.

"My name is Avery," she stated in a friendly fashion only to quickly shift the tone. "I do carry a knife," she said, pointing to a small pouch attached at her hip. It was probably the only material thing she owned aside from her clothes. How sad was that? It was a friendly salutation mixed with a sinister threat. She certainly was no stranger to potential danger.

It was an odd beginning to a lasting friendship.

She told me how she ended up on the beach and had been living on it for months. She was from a small midwest town, and she came out west to escape an abusive relationship. Her ex-boyfriend had taken everything. All of this happened when she was seventeen. Her parents were superstars of dysfunction and couldn't relate to each other, let alone their only daughter. They figured she was old enough that her prospects for a better life would be enhanced the farther away she moved. Despite the wild outward confidence, it was the vulnerability hidden beneath that beckoned me. She was not the first stray to ever wander into my world.

Ages ago, when I was maybe five or six, a kitten drifted into my yard. My parents didn't want me to keep it. I brought water and crackers for it and left a bowl near our porch each day. It would return and return, and eventually, it became part of my family. I had no brothers and sisters, and each visit was welcome company. One day, it stopped showing up in my yard and for weeks I'd wait each morning before school and until bedtime at night for its return. My mom, one evening, joined me on the steps.

"You know, Kiran, that your little friend probably won't be coming back."

"Why do you say that?"

"It's just life. People and animals grow up and move on and have to live their lives."

"Mom, I would have taken care of it. I promise I would have always taken care of it."

"Everything needs to learn to find its path and take care of itself."

I looked down at my running shoes, and I slid my tongue along my upper lip. Somehow I did comprehend my mom's message: Freedom was the greatest gift you can give any living thing.

"Everyone needs to learn to let go at some point." She smiled, but her lips trembled in doing so. "Yes. One day even I'll have to." She patted me on the head. "What you did do was wonderful for your kitten. Giving it love and letting go is never easy. You'll be rewarded for it one day. I'm sure of that."

It was as thoughtful and profound as any words my mom would ever have for me. She was a doer, so the phrases she said to me, though scarce, I preserved in my subconscious.

The words simmered up to the surface as I thought about Avery. The irony was that over time, I wondered whether it was I who truly found Avery or whether it was she who found me. The details became murky, which suited my recounting of the meeting.

I would see Avery every night on the beach for the next

week and offer her the extra food I bought nearby. We would sit and talk. The nights were getting seasonally cooler, and I had, in that short time, come to care for Avery like the sister I never had. Finally, nights later, I could take no more and convinced her to stay at my place. I slept on the couch, and the company and conversation were most enjoyable. There was something about taking care of her that gave me purpose.

The situation couldn't last forever. Friends at work wondered who the strange young woman was living with me. Neighbors cast wary glances every time we walked in and out of the apartment. Avery felt very guilty about being dependent on me. I was entirely selfish, as it was nice to have someone to talk to and share meals with. Feeling needed could be selfish, and I basked in it for as long as I could.

Time passed and eventually I found her an internship with one of my clients. Avery saved enough money to move into an apartment down the hall from me. I loaned her the initial deposit. At that point in my life, Avery truly was my sibling, even referring to me as her long-lost brother when speaking to acquaintances.

Introducing Avery to Rob, the handsome, young, up-and-comer who worked on my staff, shaped the relationship further. Within weeks, Rob moved in with Avery.

One evening, months later, Avery and Rob invited me to their apartment to announce their impending nuptials. Avery requested I be part of the wedding party. The day of the ceremony was one part joy and one part melancholy in my universe.

When they returned from their honeymoon, Avery

became my guardian. She would bring me extra food, and I would be invited to dinner with them on the odd occasion. The invites were few and far between as time passed. I could sense Rob was unnerved by the unspoken language that Avery and I seemed to share.

Rob switched firms, yet still drew upon me for advice. Avery worked from home now and, not only took care of their apartment, but also checked on me to make sure I took care of my plants. We both knew she came by just to make sure I was alive. Often I would catch her eyes roaming around my minimalist apartment. I could tell she was distressed by my isolation and wished one day she would come by to see signs of life beyond the potted plants.

CHAPTER 5

Rob was forever punctual. He was five years younger than me. He was tall with curly black hair and a lean physique. He could easily play beach volleyball and not look out of place in any photoshoot. He was also frustratingly ambitious. He sought my advice and knowledge about everything and anything. He saw in me a reservoir that he could tap and not worry about leaving anything for me. I didn't mind. He was kind to Avery, and I could tell he loved her in his way. He believed building his career and providing for her was the way to show love. And I knew that security was important for her. Rob kept me close, as he needed my experience. He also knew if I were in good spirits, Avery would worry less.

One day Rob arrived early at my door to take me to work. He told me he had an early morning meeting, but I could tell he was lying. He was wearing his usual lucky tie—one he wore at his "deal closer" meetings. He was bounding with enthusiasm. "What's with you, Tigger?" I asked semi-mockingly, as we wheeled out of the parking garage.

A smile crossed his face. "I heard old man Carson is retiring from your firm."

"Rob, you left a year ago. Who told you?"

"I have my sources."

"And what else did your sources tell you?"

"They're going to make you a partner, Kiran. Finally! You're going to take over his practice." He looked over at me as he drove, measuring my reaction.

"I didn't apply to be a partner." My brows caved in. There was a detailed process in applying for the position. You had to want it and build a comprehensive business case with the support and references from other partners. Those who applied spent lunch hours and evenings at squash courts, golf courses, anywhere senior partners were, trying to win their support. I decided a long time ago to stand on the curb as the traffic whizzed by in this insane race and, if lucky, not get clipped by a stray tire.

"Apply or not, they're going to give it to you."

"Shit. When?" I knew as soon as I said it that Rob would react, and I had to stifle the potential insult in my reaction. "I mean, I wasn't expecting it," I quickly added.

"It's meant to be a surprise. It'll come to fruition shortly after his retirement party in early June."

I faked extreme satisfaction and thanked him for the news. Way down inside, a knife tore through me, at first in a circular motion and then clanked against my now hollow interior back the other way. I wondered when I got home that evening if there was anything left to cut out, as the pulp had been consumed from the inside out long ago.

When Rob and I arrived back at the apartment complex later, Avery was waiting in the hallway with a worried look on her face.

"Everything okay, sweetie?" Rob asked.

Avery could be a good liar—except when her eyes betrayed her.

"The postman made a mistake and delivered this letter to our address." Since that often happened at our apartment building, it normally wouldn't be worthy of discussion. However, Avery's face told an uncomfortable tale as she leaned forward to hand me the letter. Her eyes were transfixed on mine as if to record my reaction before and after seeing it. No one wrote personal letters anymore it seemed, and this did not appear to be a business solicitation or a windfall from a Nigerian oil property.

"Yeah. Just a letter. Probably my old man." I knew I was wrong because my dad never wrote.

"Look at the return address." Her eyes widened with concern.

I looked at the top left-hand corner. There was no street address. Just: *Pauley River*.

"Geez."

Rob looked confused.

"It's from his hometown," Avery explained, looking at him with eyebrows raised.

Over the years, Avery and I shared little about our personal histories other than what we felt comfortable discussing. We both had reached the west coast to escape. Avery knew where I came from and how I left after graduating from college. She knew how I almost died and how there were memories buried way down below. It was simple in some ways because I couldn't remember much of that part of my life. We both agreed to move forward and leave the past as discarded litter on a deserted road.

I took the letter and started walking into my apartment.

Avery cautiously followed, as did Rob. They were going to stay close by until I opened it, and there was obviously no place to run and hide. I ripped it open nervously. There wasn't much inside. Brownish, yellowish paper slowly floated to the ground as I shook the envelope. It was an old newspaper clipping. Looking down on it as it lay on my floor, I sensed the ink waiting to stain my fingers.

As I picked it up and looked at the date, it paralyzed me. Without even reading the article, a feeling of foreboding overwhelmed me. Avery saw my reaction and pulled the paper out of my hand, almost ripping it.

Local Boy Drowns, Another in Critical Condition
Last night, an unnamed local boy is believed to have drowned in the Pauley River and another, who appears to have tried to save him, is in the hospital in critical condition. A third boy was found along the bank of the river uninjured. The circumstances of the accident and tragedy are unknown. The names are withheld due to their ages.

Avery looked at me with the most sorrowful look.

"You're the boy in critical condition?"

The hesitation before my next words lasted what felt like an eternity. It was almost as if I tried to think of some fantastic lie to tell her. In truth, my head only spun like a cheap traveling carnival ride riddled with evil clown images and spooky music. I was hoping to distract myself and awaken in a distant place. No such luck. "Yeah. The boy in critical condition was me, unfortunately."

"That's when you lost your memory," Rob added with his lips pressed together as if satisfied in connecting the large dots.

"Yep. I was in a coma for a few weeks."

"So you can't remember anything?"

"Not really," I said in an agitated voice, trying to stifle further inquiry. I took the newspaper clipping out of Avery's hand. "Bits and pieces here and there. I suppose it's best not to remember and, after all, here I am."

She whispered to Rob. "Who the fuck would send this to him?"

"I can hear you, Avery," I said laughing, trying to break the tension. "I have no idea. It was so long ago."

"What are you supposed to do?" Avery asked rhetorically.

"Nothing," I said. "It was a long time ago. It was a very tragic event, and there isn't a return address. Maybe it's just a bad joke. If someone wanted to reach me, they would have left a return address or even called or emailed."

I saw the look on Rob and Avery's faces. Rob was genuinely confused. He didn't know very much about my past and never was interested in asking. He was always forward-looking and focused, which was exactly what Avery needed.

"Seriously. I'm fine. It's been an eventful day and quiet time would do me wonders."

Avery looked at Rob. "We understand. Damn it, Kiran. If you need anything, we're down the hall."

"I know, and that's very comforting. But you guys just got married. You don't need me bumming you out."

Rob's eyes sparkled. "Umm . . . besides, there is good news.

Pretty soon Kiran will be a partner."

Avery looked at me and our eyes met. She knew there was no happiness in my eyes nor joy. She also knew of our agreement, and she didn't pursue it. Our pasts were our pasts. The anchors were too heavy to drop onto one another to carry.

I went into my apartment and lay back on the couch and stared at the ceiling all night. *Who sent me this? Why now?* It was just the beginning. It was the first of a long trolley line of sleepless nights.

The newspaper clipping made its way around my apartment. Next to my bed on the nightstand one evening. On the fridge for the next two. Everywhere except the blue recycling bin. I couldn't throw it out. Avery and Rob thought I had dismissed it since I never spoke of it. But it preoccupied my days and nights for the next couple of weeks. In the back of my mind was the date of Mr. Carson's retirement and how, if Rob was right, I would be made partner. It was not a bloodletting ceremony, of course. To me, in some ways, it was much worse.

It was late May and the California days grew warmer exponentially. Each morning, I would look in the mirror and examine myself. The darker tone around my eyes had expanded, and I was gaunt. Rob never noticed. Without a doubt, I knew Avery would, so I avoided her in any way I could.

Who would send me a news clipping from twenty years ago, without a name or a message or some other clue? I worked long hours to avoid being alone at home with my thoughts during this time. That article was always nearby and begging me for investigation. I looked at it again carefully, even subjecting it to a small magnifying glass. There were no handwritten notes or messages attached. All the way here across the continent, I was safe from everything but my mind.

One day about a week or two later, there was a rare late afternoon shower as I arrived home. I picked up my mail from the box, and there was an envelope there. This time, there was no return address. As soon as I touched it, my hand trembled, somehow connecting to some unseen force. I quickly tucked it under my shirt and retreated to my apartment before Avery or Rob would notice.

It sat on my kitchen table. It was a solitary rectangle on my round wood table. It wasn't standard envelope size. For sure it was no regular junk mail. I shivered from the heavy dampness of the clothes against my skin as my air conditioning took effect. I left the room to change and was drawn back in by the letter. It sat there patiently waiting for my return.

I finally summoned some courage and slowly tore it open with my fingers. I could see that there was one page on the inside: old-style loose-leaf paper with discernible blue ink. My heart pulsated, almost exploding. I pulled out the folded paper and unraveled it. The paper had clearly been water-damaged and was rough where it had been wet. There was a brownish yellow staining around it as though touched by the earth. I froze, paralyzed even before I read the first line. It was rarer nowadays that someone wrote by hand. Despite that, there was one thing I could quickly decipher, albeit from years ago. The handwriting was my own. I was startled and almost screamed. I closed my eyes and prayed it would go away until I read the first line and saw the form the letter took. I was too overwhelmed to move. It was a poem and in my distinctive handwriting dressed in blue ink. A poem that should not have existed anymore found life suddenly. My hands trembled as I stared at the letter. A bright light was shining on my past. My memory remained hidden in a chasm desperately trying not to be exposed. It was mine, but I refused to accept it.

The next thing I knew I awoke to a knock on my apartment door. It was just after 11 p.m. I had blacked out. The first blackout episode in a long time. I had been masterful at staying in between the lines for so long that the foray outside the perimeter overcame my atrophic mind.

It was Rob and Avery.

Rob looked at me. "You seem out of sorts. Why didn't you come to our place for dinner?"

"I must have fallen asleep."

Avery walked around me. Her eyes were darting across the room with the buzz of a dying fly. She could sense something was not right. I had tucked away the letter into my pocket. There was no way I was showing them this. They would send me for tests. Years ago, I was warned that due to the memory loss there could be occasions when I blacked out and forgot more recent events. My doctor said I should keep track of it. I didn't. It hadn't happened in so long. I had been strong enough to keep the door shut and not let my mind wander outside of the cell I had built for it.

Rob looked around the room smiling, having moved on

from my mystery and to the point as always. "Tomorrow is the Carson retirement party, right? Have they said anything to you yet?"

"Yes. I meant to tell you. McCastle scheduled a meeting with me next week. He said it was important." Mac McCastle was the managing partner of our firm. You either saw him when you were being fired or promoted.

"Ah!" Rob laughed. "I'm sure that's when they'll tell you. Congrats."

Avery looked at Rob with her brow arched ever so slightly. "Rob, you totally spoiled his surprise!" She was annoyed that Rob had distracted the conversation from my plight.

I stopped Avery before she could say more. "No, Avery, it's okay. I hate surprises."

"I suppose so." Avery stared at my face. "You were sleeping, right? It looks like you haven't slept in days." Avery zeroed in and would not let go. For someone so young, she was very in tune with peeling away false expressions of normalcy.

"Totally fine, Avery. I've just had a bad cold and kept to myself."

They brought me leftovers and stayed with me for the next hour. All Rob could talk about was my imminent promotion. Avery just stared at me with a perplexed look. Meanwhile, the letter ate away at my pocket as it slowly made its way into my head where it would surely take root, burn through my skin, and strangle my heart for one last time.

Over the next few days, I came very close to putting the letter into the recycling with the usual junk mail. I never found the courage. I handled the letter in my hand so often that I cut myself on one of the edges at one point. A smear of blood mixed in with the ink. Finally, with a labored gasp, I slipped the two pieces of mail into a drawer and tried to forget about them.

Something about it was very obviously wrong. Two letters, one with a cryptic handwritten return address, the other with none, both coming as ghosts from a time years ago buried in dust. Every day I would check if there was more mail or anything else. I took longer and longer walks along the beach.

One night a storm cloud gathered off the coast. I could see the evening skies losing light quickly. There were rarely tornadoes here but the winds had picked up dramatically, and a strong gust hit me and knocked me off balance. For a second, it was as though the sun disappeared and there was nothing except black clouds. I ran in and closed the windows, fast expecting a heavy rain that never came. The sun eventually returned. The fear remained. My whole world grew more sinister. I never knew black existed in so many shades.

The sleepless nights continued. It started with my breathing becoming more and more rapid. Thoughts raced in and out of my mind. Images, faces—mostly ones I didn't recognize— paraded before me. The ones circling in my mind were erased so quickly that I couldn't identify them; I only sensed they were familiar and threatening. I often went to the washroom to cool my face off with a cold cloth.

Rob saw my nervousness and assumed I was anxious for my upcoming meeting with Mr. McCastle. I had done millions of business meetings and never lost sleep over them.

Besides, I should be happy. I was going to be a big-cheese partner. Sometimes your cheese just does not get moved when you need it. The worse part was to come.

Two nights before my big meeting, I could feel the air sucked out of my lungs by some unseen force. My nose was blocked up as my breathing became more labored. I leaped out of bed and paced, making each breath more heroic and desperate. Finally, I ran outside into the summer night. The open space in front of me pacified my nerves and calmed my breathing.

I realized when I went back to bed that an hour had passed. I knew it was a panic attack that seemingly went on forever. I was grateful it was over. You can indeed drown and not even get wet.

More disconcerting to me was the mystery sender. Night after night, I would hold the article and poem in my hands and gaze. A tug of war ensued in my mind with my heart in the middle. Whichever side won, it would be a defeat for me. The nightmares were more like a knocking on my door day in and day out as I tried to ignore them. These dreams were bits and pieces of black confetti falling on my mind. They were absent of color, threatening and sinister. They were filling up every empty void in me. Eventually, they would suffocate me. I only knew as much because of how I felt when I awoke: tired and in a perpetual struggle for air. My past awaited its victory.

CHAPTER 6

It was less than forty-eight hours before the meeting with Mac McCastle, the managing partner at Beckett and Bells Investments LLP. I fidgeted in bed, with eyes wide open and unflinching, staring at the ceiling. The moon painted my room in its ancient light. I had forgotten how powerful the moonlight could be on a clear evening. I tried to baptize myself in it.

The comfort I felt was short-lived as my thoughts surrendered to the present and my fear. The upcoming meeting and the letters tugged and poked at me. I slowly sat up and took an elongated inhale. I may have held my breath not for a brief second, nor ten or even twenty. Maybe if I stopped breathing I could go into suspended animation. It didn't escape me that I had in fact been in a coma and nearly turned the trick once before.

A vision of my future swept in as unsympathetic as a prairie winter wind dusting every hair follicle with an icy caress. I realized I needed to pour coats and coats of hard lacquer over me to focus on the one thing that was known: They were going to make me a partner. Clearly, Rob had pulled all his strings. He had become a bright, ambitious, and well-thought-of man in the industry. I had no doubt this was his gift to me for the years of friendship and mentoring, not to mention introducing him to Avery.

If I focused on this meeting as an objective, I could keep the chains moving and run out the clock. Maybe the past would forget me. I resolved to make a go of it and started concentrating on the interview questions I would need to answer. Rob prepared notes and left them in my apartment. He was ever helpful, undoubtedly hoping to draw me further into his vision of success. I finally found them near the half-open window just as a spider had slowly started its web along the top of the pane. I picked up the notes, handling them as one would clutch a virus-laden tissue, and then scrutinized the question-and-answer style format. Bullshit. More bullshit and then real bullshit.

Suddenly, I noticed the spider crawling on the back of my hand. My left hand instinctively rose to strike and end its existence. As my hand reached up ever so slightly, I just as slowly lowered it back down. The spider both fascinated and hypnotized me.

I could feel the gentle bite and its syrupy poison slithering into my flesh. I did nothing other than move my hand to the open window and let it continue crawling to safety, nourished by my blood.

The wind picked up, causing Rob's notes to curl in my hand. Eventually, I succumbed to the pain and itch and my fingers shook. All of Rob's tirelessly complete notes fluttered across the room like crazed moths released into a bright beacon. The moonlight invaded through my open window led by a beam of laser-like light darting across the chamber. The ray of light settled on the paper by my nightstand, illuminating it. The letter glistened like a diamond—the one containing the poem. I stared at it for an instant. The thought of what I could no longer avoid energized me. The newfound resolve I felt shook me. A burning bush would not have provided more clarity.

I walked across the room to my door. It was almost 4 a.m. I put on a white T-shirt and blue sneakers. The knot in the laces that I had been too lazy to undo stared back at me. I got up in victory. I walked down the hall and the back stairs of the apartment complex to the recycling bins. I took all of Rob's notes and prep questions and unceremoniously dropped them in. While I walked back to my apartment, I looked up at the full moon. I could feel my lungs fill with air and, for, the first time in years, I closed my eyes in silent prayer, albeit briefly. I went back up to my place to look for my storage key. Years ago, when I moved here, I had put one item away in the common storage area. It was the only thing I kept from my past.

I raced far into the back of the basement, rifling through other tenants' boxes upon boxes of old clothes. Finally, I got to the only box I had long ago hidden deep within this cave. It was far enough to forget about it, yet safe enough to be secure from certain disposal. I dusted off the cardboard cover and slowly lifted it off. When I opened the box, it lay right before me: a NASA flight jacket.

A rush of emotions hit me at once. Looking at it was like peering into another lifetime and another world. The memory came at me hard and fast.

It was the much-heralded first day of our senior year. I hadn't thought about what to wear, and settled on a plain blue cotton T-shirt accompanied by a faded pair of blue jeans. My sneakers were well worn and comfortable. The girls would surely start the first day dressed to the hilt.

I stopped at the mirror that sat perched menacingly on the small oak dresser. Did I dare look? No teenager could resist the temptation. I seemed dull. Different shades of blue and no radio this year. I felt naked. I could barely hear my dad's voice as he left for work. My mom had long since left, as her shift at the bakery started at 4 a.m.

"Kiran, I left you something on the table to buy lunch. PLEASE DO NOT FORGET!" He must have called out numerous times; he was at top volume.

"Sure, thanks, Dad," I said.

I hurried down the stairs and found toast. There was some coffee left in the pot. There was enough for a cup. My parents didn't like me drinking coffee in the morning and didn't know I had been doing it for the last year. It was half milk that I drank. I emptied out the pot so they would never know how much I guzzled.

I saw an envelope right next to a carton of milk, so I wouldn't miss it. Strange. My dad or mom usually left cash for me to buy lunch, but never put it in an envelope. It wasn't sealed, so I could make out that there was something else inside beside a ten-dollar bill.

"Kiran, we left you money for lunch. Please go in the closet in front before you leave. A little something for your last year in high school. Your dad chose it. Love, Mom."

I frowned and wondered what it was they left for me in the closet. I could only assume the worst. It was some dreaded sweater or shoes they picked out for me. They tried....

I was floored when I opened the front entrance closet. The lining underneath was almost a bright orange. It had a wool collar, the exterior was made of nylon, and it was water repellent. The color was blue. My eyes were attracted to the patch of the Orion star system and the unmistakable "NASA" lettering over the right breast. On the left side was the mission patch with an eagle and the word "Apollo." It was the NASA flight jacket my dad had seen me eyeing when I wandered off into some thrift shop months ago.

I remembered seeing it hanging on the wall. I had gone in looking to buy a bomber jacket to replace the fighter one that was way too big for me, but the price was way beyond what I had saved up. The flight jacket had caught my eye on my way out. While I gently ran my fingers across the patch, he snuck up beside me.

"Well, you wanted to be an astronaut."

"Aw, that was when I was just a kid. Besides, it costs a lot more than I have," I said as I dismissively waved my fingers at it and walked out the door ahead of my dad.

Fricken f'ing awesome. Here it was. How cool was that?! I quickly tried it on and discovered it fit perfectly. I realized at this point that I had better hurry up. I quickly grabbed a pen and scribbled on the envelope.

"Mom and Dad, thanks. It's great. Thank you so much."

My mom sighed when I came home. "Well, thankfully it fits and looks better than the last jacket you had."

I let the past wash over me as I eyed the jacket. The only possession remaining from my youth looked as it did years ago. I knew I needed to go back. Something was waiting for me. A foreboding came over me, dressed in the gaudiest of fear. I was startled by the strength of the emotion welling up inside. I didn't understand. *Why after all these years?* I had carefully placed locks, chains, and walls around my memories. Someone was prying them open one by one, and it was not me. I couldn't understand who was trying to get in. I just needed to get out before they opened the last lock and got to me.

The moon sending its light to shine on the letter was a sigil sent from my past. I needed to find my way back to the source.

I slowly walked upstairs and quietly down the hall, retreating to my apartment. I didn't sleep a wink that night and fought my way through waves of panic attacks that lasted briefly only to return when I thought the worst was over.

By dawn, I had walked the neighborhood for more than an hour to calm myself down. It was also a way of saying goodbye to a place I must surely leave.

The couch in my living room became my base camp. It was now almost 5:30 a.m. Usually, I left for work by 6:30 a.m. and in Los Angeles traffic got into the office by 7:30. Rob would often come by, and we would carpool.

I gently tapped on Rob's door. He should be up already.

"You're early."

"Yeah. You're on your own today, Rob."

"You good?"

"Yes. Just taking the day off to prepare for the interview."

"Good idea. Get some rest, too. You look like shit."

"Thanks. I will." As he closed the door, I could hear him muttering something to Avery. He quickly reopened the door.

"Kiran. I totally forgot. Avery reminded me. I'm flying out tonight for a client meeting in San Francisco tomorrow. You'll have to fend for yourself in the morning." Typical Rob, short and to the point.

"No problem."

"Good luck with the meeting tomorrow! Call me once the meeting is done. Promise?"

"Sure, Rob. You'll be the first to know how it goes." *Sure, Rob. Good luck.*

He closed the door, and I went back to my apartment. The moon had disappeared and its glow was eaten by rising sun.

I got more done on this day than I had in a lifetime. I prepared notes for Avery about the plants that needed watering. I made sure all the bills were paid and up to date. Most importantly, I made a one-way flight reservation. Rob would not be back for a day or so and, by then, it would be too late to stop me.

That night Rob came to see me before his flight to wish me luck again. Avery offered to make me a meal. I refused and told them I needed to be alone to get into the right mindset for my meeting.

When midnight finally came, I packed a laundry bag with every suit and tie I owned, except one set of clothes. I put on a pair of black beach trunks, a white T-shirt, and sandals. I tiptoed out of the apartment, turned a corner, and walked the three blocks to the beach. I found a quiet spot away from any curious night-owl tourists, laundry bag in tow.

Emptying the contents of clothing onto the sandy beach, I waited for the waves to come close and take these items away for good. When the tide moved closer to the pile, the beauty of the ocean wrapped its mouth around my brain in a sweet embrace. I quickly grabbed the clothes and raced far from the water. I ran down side streets and back alleys until I found a spot in a dark crevice of a street. I threw the clothes out of the bag and left them in the alley. Hopefully, someone could put them to use.

I returned to the beach, free at last, and waded in, going farther and farther. When I got deep into the water, I could feel the cuddling of waves, first around my thighs and then my waist and then my shoulders. A voice suddenly called from behind me.

"Son! Do not go out too much farther. If a strong current comes in, you could be in trouble and there are no lifeguards at this hour."

I looked back and noticed someone about forty feet away. I could see the outline, sculpted out of the moon's glow, of an older woman. I walked back toward her and to the shore.

"Sorry. I was just daydreaming. I mean night dreaming. You're right; the waves can be dangerous."

She had gray hair. Most striking were her hazel-colored eyes. She was about seventy or so and in decent shape for her age, despite the wrinkles. Her glare was scalding.

"Out here kind of late, aren't you?" She was squinting at me, seemingly unsure of what she was seeing.

"I was thinking the same thing," I said, laughing.

"Well, I come out here every night. My husband and I used to come here every night once we retired."

"Where is he?" Just as the words tumbled out of my mouth, I knew the answer and felt sheepish for asking.

"He passed away a year ago," she said stoically.

"I'm so sorry."

"Don't be. He's still always with me."

My head tilted as I tried to understand. She caught my cue and elaborated.

"When he was dying, he told me I could always find him in the moonlight, here on the beach, his favorite place."

"That's sweet," I said with a smile. "It is a peaceful place. The ocean and the sky. I'm out here often. It reassures me, in a way."

"And what are you hoping to find out here in the moonlight at this hour? A young man, out here alone."

"Nothing." I paused and instantly knew the pause was far too long. "Really, I like thinking out here."

"Young men do not just come out here to the beach and almost drown themselves unless they are looking for *something*." She had a confident look in her eyes.

"No, seriously. I just like coming here to think and relax. I lost myself in the calmness of the water and went out too far."

She sighed as if about to scold a petulant child, but then she seemed to think better of it. "It's getting a little late, and, at my age, you get tired pretty fast." She stifled a yawn. "Good luck," she said as she started to walk away.

"Thanks and have nice night."

She looked over her shoulder at me, turned around, and came walking back toward me. She obviously couldn't hold back the thoughts attempting to escape.

"I hope you find her."

My eyes widened and my heart started beating wildly as I felt a tremor within me, an unleashing of a dormant hungry force.

"I think you know what I mean. I hope you find her." She turned and walked back away from the shore, having made very clear what her message was by repeating it.

I stood watching her, thinking about what she said. I stared at the moon and sky and closed my eyes. "Find her???" I said to myself out loud. A soft droplet trickled down my cheek and then another and then another, and I thought a splash of water must have hit my eyes.

It hadn't happened in so long that I couldn't recognize my own tears. Wading back to shore, I fell briefly asleep outside the reach of the ocean; my face glazed by my eyes' salty acid. The angels must have carried me back to my apartment that night, for I have no recollection of ever leaving the beach.

CHAPTER 7

I awoke in my bed just as the sun rose. It levitated in a beautiful orange aura. It seemed exceptionally bright, even embracing. I took it to mean that my plans had acceptance. My effort to convince myself was indeed valiant. Within an instant, I could see storm clouds forming far off on the horizon. Even though I knew they would never reach the shore, it was unsettling. My subconscious, I believed, summoned them to warn me. My fists clenched with resolve. There would be no turning back today. Running through an elaborate perpetual maze being chased by a tireless adversary had exhausted me of this game. No longer would I be the hunted, although the choice appeared to have been mine all along.

I got up, grabbed my car keys and wallet and made my way through my apartment complex. The coarse sand crystals irritated my toes, remnants of my late night walk. My clothes were carefully selected. I wore the one remaining suit and tie still in my possession. They were pardoned the preceding night for one final tour of duty. In the briefcase I carried was a change of clothes and a formally crafted letter. My movements were quick and quiet. I was desperate to ensure Avery did not hear me. Within an instant, I was in my car.

***

At 9:05 a.m, I entered the premises of Beckett and Bells LLP and made my way to the infamous corner office of Mr. Mac McCastle. There were snickers and some staring as I walked into his chambers. I had arrived five minutes late. It was fashionably late on a regular day but today was the day of my big meeting so being late was scandalous. I gave a customary nod of acknowledgment to his administrative assistant and swooped in.

Mr. McCastle was no doubt expecting me. He was finishing a phone call as I walked in and sought refuge in the oversized and uncomfortable chair in front of him. The Mr. McCastle. The man who had fired many colleagues of mine because their flaw was a lack of commitment to the firm. Firm first, family second. He was the judge and juror of my world. He put his cell phone down with zeal to send a message that I had annoyed him. He had a grim look on his face and made it a point to look at his watch.

"I know this is the West Coast, Wells. Come on, man, five minutes late! You know how much I bill per hour?" He was only half joking.

It was customary, or so I heard, for him to set the tone immediately during a meeting. There could be no doubt who the predator and the prey were. I surveyed his desk and surroundings. The traditional family photos sat strategically placed, although everyone in the office knew the old man was never home. Probably had never been to any one of his children's activities. His habitat was the golf course or some other corporate event. He was always looking to bring in new business. He made it to the top ranks knowing people. Actually, knowing the *right* people. In his wake was a body count requiring scientific notation to track. Rob belonged to the same country club as him. I declined to join, citing a need to focus on my work years ago. With no family waiting at home, there was nothing to come in second anyway. The firm quickly formed that perception which made me valuable.

Without making an excuse, I just sat vacantly smiling at him as if I had no idea I was even mildly late. My hand smoothed my tie, waiting for his next move. Sure enough, he could not keep silent for too long, and his paw stretched out across his desk and reached for a file at its edge. It was as he lifted out from his seat when I realized the secret to his magic. His chair was propped up inches higher than mine, giving him the advantage of an illusion of grandeur. No matter how he sat in that chair, he would be talking down to me. Capturing a glimpse of his insecurity, I smiled to myself.

"Are you in a good mood, Wells? You should be. You should be, young man." He reclined back in his chair, and it was evident he wasn't interested in having a two-way conversation. He didn't wait for a response, nor did he even give me the courtesy of the fake expression of interest. Small talk was never time well spent in his world. I worked for him. I was not a client, so the witty repartee of a conversation carried no value.

He opened the file and laughed as he spoke of my impressive credentials and recapped my professional history going back to my university education. He talked about all the billable hours, the commitment I made regarding travel whenever the firm needed me, and of all my performance reviews. The names of the clients I had worked on and how much money the firm had billed on all of these trickled from his tongue. He then mentioned how Rob had lobbied him at the country club for the past year. Rob apparently told him I would do anything for the firm and how committed I was to its success. This betrayal I absorbed in stride because today I would have the final say. The diatribe took a turn just as my patience to sit and listen was waning.

Mr. McCastle put the file down and stared at me. He then proceeded to tell me point-blank how he opposed my being promoted to partner because I lacked the social and networking skills for such a venerable position. He doubted I would be able to bring in new business. New business was needed to keep the blood flowing in this corporate body. Then, of course, came that moment that was supposed to make him the friendly teddy bear of a leader. He would support my promotion regardless because I was the consummate team player. His exact term was "good soldier." I grinned when he turned that phrase. The smile was not because it carried substantive meaning to me. Good soldiers tended to get shot first. The irony amused me. The words were my starter's pistol.

I began to stare in earnest at the gold business card holder perched near the front of his desk. It was pointed directly at me and to any visitor in this office. As he took a pause to suck seemingly whatever air remained in the room for himself, I slowly leaned over and plucked one of the cards out of the placeholder and began admiring it. My hands cupped it while my fingers caressed it almost seductively. He stared at me, bewildered.

"Excellent quality paper, sir. Very alluring." I then muttered to myself in envious disgust and made darn sure he heard. Each syllable was in tune to a stroke of a finger on the card. "Even better than my card. A bit too much better." I looked up at his befuddled expression and placed the card back in the holder.

My eyes reached out to him as I asked to leave for a break. I described to him my coffee habit and the need to relieve myself. I shifted my legs at different angles to emphasize the point and unnerve him. I mentioned, as the icing on the cake, my desire to call my girlfriend to tell her the great news as soon as possible. All lies, of course.

He looked up and smiled and in an officious tone replied, "Please hurry up. I have an out-of-office meeting at 11 a.m." For a second, I thought he said "out-of-body experience" and giggled. Now *that* would be a meeting not to miss.

I quickly grabbed my briefcase and, fleet of foot, headed straight for the washroom outside of the reception area. He was visibly confused about my taking the briefcase with me. Luckily, he was too self-absorbed with wiping the smudges off his business card holder to appreciate the strangeness of my actions.

Entering into the closest stall I could find, I shed the skin I had worn for the better part of the last fifteen years: dress socks, oxford shoes, jacket, tie, shirt, and pants. I opened my briefcase and pulled out my casual wardrobe: a midnight blue plaid shirt with black squares, blue jeans, white socks, sneakers, and, of course, a T-shirt underneath. Not just any T-shirt. I gathered up all my business attire and stuffed them into the briefcase before shoving everything into the garbage of the washroom.

When I walked out of the washroom, I proceeded directly to the main reception where Denise stood watch. Denise and I started at the firm within a year of one another—I'd known her for years. The stunned look on her face said it all. She suddenly realized what would be happening next when I handed her my formal resignation letter. No way was I going to give this to Mr. McCastle directly, as I refused to allow him to get close to me. He did have massive hands, which were easy to imagine morphing into battering ram fists.

"Kiran. I knew this day would come. I knew it," she said, laughing and shaking her head as she took the envelope from me. Perhaps there were betting odds in the administrative staff lunch area, unknown to me. I wondered sometimes.

"One favor, Denise. Just one."

"Sure."

"If the old geezer asks you to call security, just give me a head start until I'm in the elevator."

She chuckled. "For sure. Sometimes the phone line goes down at really inopportune times." As I was about to walk away, she added, "Good luck. We'll miss you."

"Thanks. I appreciate it."

I lowered my head and walked around the fake privacy of the cubicle world and curious faces. Many probably thought

I was heading to the beach and forgot something in my office. We were in California, after all. I marched past McCastle's secretary with a gracious nod and a wink. His face almost instantaneously turned beet red the moment I re-entered his chamber.

"Wells! What the hell did you change for? This is so unprofessional. Our meeting ends when I say it's over." He was so incredulous, he managed the energy to stand up so he could attempt to talk down to me.

"I don't have much time. There's a letter for you at Denise's desk. Good luck on your future endeavors, sir."

"What? Have you been drinking? Did you go out to celebrate already and not invite me?" He laughed menacingly at his joke, trying to convince himself that this was an orchestrated prank on himself. He was a narcissist to the end.

"I don't work for you anymore," I said, smirking. "You seem to be having trouble understanding." Making sure not to cross the threshold again, I stood in the entrance of his office. There was no way I was going to have the door close behind me and run the risk of not being able to escape readily. My flight ticket was non-refundable, just in case I was tempted to change my plans.

"What the fuck? Are you joking?" He let out a strange nervous laugh, the anger about to spew forth. He leaned forward and stared at my T-shirt.

"Oh. You like my shirt? It's one of my favorite bands; you must have heard of them." I knew there was no way.

"Sonic Youth? For God's sake, Wells. You're going to be forty in a couple of years, and you're wearing this teenage crap!"

I laughed. "Actually, sir, they're older than me, and I've been listening to them since I was a teen. They make great music even at your age. Imagine that!" I laughed in an entirely exaggerated tone. I took one small step backward, starting to turn away. The gas gushed into that office with my words, and all that was left was the ignition. In a low distinctive tone, I started singing and accentuated the lyrics as I turned to face him one last time. I doubt he knew the lyrics to "Teenage Riot". I did not care. I was singing them to myself.

He didn't have the courage to move toward me and confront me as he was already on the phone to reception dropping f-bombs on poor Denise. I closed the door behind myself just after saluting him while continuing my song. Good soldier indeed. I couldn't help myself and reopened the door briefly. "You know, I can order you a T-shirt, too, if you'd like. They do come in your size, big guy!" Before his face could change colors again, I was gone.

An explosion of verbal assaults ricocheting across the office commenced. I wondered how quickly he would call Rob. Rob's reaction would be almost as priceless.

I thought of my friends who'd had their careers ended after going into McCastle's office —people who had kids and families who depended on them—and a hint of retribution stretched across my face in the form of a smirk as the daggers and bombs of his words flew at me from his corporate box of an office. I made my way down the hallways, passing smaller offices. Focused and alert in my quest to escape, I met each face I passed with a nod.

Making my way through the mazes of gray cabinets, filled with files, tucked away in a tone of self-importance, I didn't look back until I reached reception and noticed Denise bravely holding back the smile that was tickling the corners of her mouth. The phone next to her buzzed loudly with lights flashing, all calls forwarded to a voicemail that couldn't care less. She looked up at me. "You know what would have been a nice touch?"

"What?"

"Signing the visitor's log Patrick Bateman." She winked at me while nodding at the paper in front.

"Now, Denise. That would have been a little too over the top! Besides, he's probably never even read the book or seen the movie." I waved at her, picking up my pace.

With each floor I descended, the sweet smell of my career incinerating behind me was intoxicating. There was no turning back now.

I made my way to my car and was back at my apartment soon enough. There was one more person who potentially could stop me: Avery. I prayed she wouldn't be home and if so, wouldn't see me. I also knew it wouldn't be long before Rob found out. I pictured him on his Blackberry, then dropping his Blackberry as the text came in.

I went into my apartment and clutched the bags I had packed the day before and seized my plane ticket. The note I had left for Avery on the kitchen table was now sitting next to a plant on the countertop. Avery was too thorough and reliable. She'd already been in here to water my plants. She knew. She definitely knew.

I raced my way out of the apartment with everything I wanted to take with me. My car waited patiently, a willing accomplice in my escape. After I turned the corner, I could see a silhouette sitting on the hood. My heart sank. I knew who it was without seeing her clearly.

"Good thing I went to water your plants or else I would never have been able to see you."

"It's too hard to explain, Avery."

"Rob called me already. You know that, right?"

"I kind of figured. How mad was he?"

"Pissed."

"One day I'll explain it to him."

"No. I will."

She stared at me with an intensity I've never seen before. "You're going back home, aren't you? That stupid article you received?"

"Another letter came."

"Christ. I knew something was going on. I can go with you." She reached out her hand and tried to grab my wrist. I politely pulled it back and out of her grasp.

"No. You need to be with Rob. My past is something I have to confront. I can't drag you into it."

"You almost died once, Kiran!"

"You have to understand why I need to go back. I promise to be careful. If I don't do anything now, I never will. Eventually, it would just eat away at me until . . . well. Get the picture?" Her sigh drifted through the air and pulsated against my eardrum. She had her past, too, and her demons. She also knew of the importance of confronting them and the false safety of not.

"Of course. It doesn't mean I won't worry. Maybe Rob and I can make a vacation out of it and come with you," she said pleadingly.

"No. Besides . . ." I reached out my other hand and gently padded her belly. A look of shock crossed her face. Her secret was exposed.

"You know?" Her lips pursed, and she slowly smiled, excited to share the moment, however bittersweet the timing was.

"Yes. Rob needs you, and you need him now. You should be enjoying the best time of your life, Avery. That's the one thing I know for sure." I moved my hand over the air above her head from shoulder to shoulder like a wand. "Keep burning bright. Understand?"

"I think so." She reached down and grabbed my hand and moved it from left to right over my head. "For good luck."

I smiled, then turned and walked around her to put my luggage in the trunk. Her voice was now barely audible, in a hushed tone. "You forgot your jacket. It gets cold back home from what you once told me." She pulled out my old flight jacket that she had hidden behind her.

"I was wondering why it wasn't in the apartment. You took it?"

"Yes. I thought maybe you would change your mind if you couldn't find it."

I stood speechless as she grinned back at me, her eyes a bright watery green. "How did you know? I mean, what made you think of it?" I asked, confused.

"Sometimes I know more than I let on, although it doesn't mean I understand it. Who gets letters? I saw the strange look on your face. I've never seen you scared before. If only I knew what they meant, I could have burnt them before you saw or read them." She continued admiring the jacket as if suddenly seeing it for the first time. "What kind of jacket is it? It doesn't look like a military-type."

"An astronaut's flight jacket."

"It's nice," she said, her eyes staring at the logo.

"Had it since high school. I'm not sure if it's real. Probably only a replica. It doesn't quite fit now, but it has sentimental value."

"Is this from one of the moon landings?" She pointed at the mission logo.

"Not sure really."

"I know there was one where the astronauts died on the launch pad. Fire devoured them. Horrible way to go. I hope it's not that one. Good karma is surely needed."

"Don't think it is that one. There was also one where they tried to go to the moon and never made it. They returned safely," I said smiling. I grabbed the jacket from her and was about to climb into the car. She lost herself in the intensity of the moment and, carried by a flood of emotion, rushed toward me. She leaned forward and grabbed my head tightly. She kissed me firmly on the forehead right above my eyes, dead center.

"This wards off evil spirits." She backed off, composing herself with her lips quivering.

"Wow. Now I'm scared. I thought you stopped believing

in all that stuff."

She backed farther away, her eyes fixed on mine. "Maybe I don't, but I know you do," she said with a forced smile and turned away.

"When do you plan to come back?" she said.

I avoided the question, like she probably knew I would, and started the car while rolling down the window. "I'll call you once I settle in and leave you a number where you can reach me. If my dad calls, don't tell him a thing. Please." I could see her waving in the distance as she gently rubbed her belly while I backed up.

My car would be abandoned temporarily in the airport lot. In my note, I asked Avery to pick it up one day and drop it off in some alleyway with the spare keys inside. I figured whoever found my clothes could use a car, too. Beckett and Bells would be hiring.

Driving to the airport, I realized how sharp and long the claws of the past were to pull me back in after so many years. For so long, I tricked myself into believing I had escaped. I could no longer hide; it had found me disguised in the form of my true love. It's amazing, the power of ink on paper.

CHAPTER 8

Pauley River, June 2006

I arrived back in Pauley River, choosing to remain in exile at the outset. Without a map or a compass before me, my next steps needed to be chosen carefully. Landmines lay everywhere—even in the friendliest of places. With my sneakers off and feet firmly on the floor, I prepared to immerse myself in water again. This time, though, it was in the sanctity of a simple bath.

The ceramic coolness of the floor did not deter my curiosity. The bath stood enticingly, waiting for me. Something about its forgotten stillness captured me at that moment. I knelt down slowly, almost reverently, and gazed at the water. I really didn't know what I was trying to do. I couldn't see my reflection in it. Not seeing it made me wonder if I existed.

I realized only later that it was the peaceful tranquility seducing me. For now, without thought or observation, I just stared at the water. I closed my eyes slowly when the words trickled through from the backlot area of my mind.

"I am here to awaken you."

My eyes opened, and I looked deeper and more nervously at the water. It remained still and tranquil. I didn't take my eyes off of the tub, wondering what magical spirit it had just conjured. I didn't need to look around the room and search for someone else there. Even though it wasn't my voice, it was a voice I had heard before, long ago muffled. I could put no face to the voice, just as I couldn't see my face within the reflected waters.

The glow from the light overhead spread like an aura from the center to the sides of the bath. I had forgotten what peace felt like or had felt like until now. I wondered what kind of sensation a hand or a finger in the water would bring. Would it be hot and would I need to pull away quickly, or would it be cold and numbing? I did not find out. The voice had tapered off to a distant memory as if hiding, hoping for a childlike game to commence. I wrapped my palms around each knee and closed my eyes again, resting. I never worried that I would fall asleep, nor did I worry about losing track of time. Time is what I owned now. No place to go, no one waiting for me. I had made a choice, right or wrong. Time was only moving slowly enough for my past to catch me eventually. Time seemed to be a patient conqueror.

I finally extended my finger into the water and "pinged" the stillness, watching impassively at the ripples I created. I amused myself for a while this way. Ripples shot out in different directions. I named a ripple for myself and watched it expand its borders before crashing into another one I created. The theory of nothing was what I sought.

The sudden ring shattered the serenity. Damn the phone. Disconnecting it was never an option. It was probably Avery. She was my only anchor and only safe harbor. My knees were numb, and one of my legs fell asleep. I enjoyed the sensation of my hand and then arm immersing itself, grasping for the plug. The ring continued at its metronomic pace. I staggered to the phone with a limp leg.

My answer of a curt "Hello" was borderline groggy, partially mixed with nighttime exhaustion. No voice responded. The old Bulova clock on the end table reminded me how long I had lingered. The clock itself was meaningless, as was the ritual of seeking it out. I knew the phone would ring again at some point, whether it would be five minutes, one hour, or days from now. I looked at the phone, almost trying to will another ring with my thoughts just to get it over with. Staring at the bath had somehow refreshed and comforted me. But I knew the worry would come back, whether it be like a lightning bolt or slowly like a boa constrictor strangling the life out of me.

The bed upon which I now sat was comfortable enough. The apartment was like many a hotel I had stayed in and had the same temporary feel. On the tired old walls there was a hint of layers of wallpaper long since removed. Someone had washed the slightly yellowed walls with a cloth as there were uneven watermarks here and there. Thankfully, the floors were dark hardwood. It was my only sticking point with the landlady. No carpeting. I was not obsessed with germs or anything, but not knowing what lurked in the recesses of a carpet's fabric was too much mystery. I made some lame excuses about allergies.

The bath held a unique charm, as I never took baths. I had gotten so accustomed to the quick get wet, get dry, get out of the house rhythm of a shower that I almost forgot what water in a tub even felt like. Now the water was totally drained. I summoned some measure of courage and decided to finally leave my humble abode and go for a walk.

I knew if I procrastinated long enough that the good intentions I had to leave the safety of isolation would be gone, but satisfactory progress was how I described my day so far. It was as though I was preparing for an eventual visit to a psychiatrist. *Yes, the patient made good progress. He filled a tub of water and emptied it.*

From the edge of the bed, I could see my reflection in the dresser mirror. Good lord, it had been a while since I shaved. I stroked my beard and remembered a time in my youth when this was the look I wished I could achieve. I laughed as I approached the mirror. The look was probably more of a washed-up folk singer than anything else. The beard took the focus away from the dusky circles under my eyes and my pale skin. Before I stopped shaving I had thought I looked jaundiced, or maybe it was shading created by unforgiving lights. The beard elegantly covered up any imperfections now. I looked healthy enough to go out without anyone worrying about me.

My success was in eating regularly, albeit only because of the kindness of my landlady. I appreciated all of the home-cooked meals I'd had in the last few years. There just was never enough time to sit down and prepare my own food. Fortunately, the landlady had brought me a welcome meal the first day I moved in. She demonstrated concern for my well-being almost from the time we met.

Within two weeks I knew that she'd been widowed for ten years, what her kids were up to, what schools they were at, who married whom, and which marriages she knew would never work. She hadn't come by as often in the last few days. I guess the allure of the new stranger had worn off and there wasn't much entertainment value in my plight—or so she thought.

Strangely, I did miss her in a way. Hearing her footsteps in her home below me was the only company I had. There was a delight she took in telling me her stories that made her smile and laugh all by herself. It was better than watching television, but I never knew what to give back in the conversation. Even the slightest hint at my past would crack the door open wide enough for her to get in. I couldn't put her through the aggravation of playing with the Russian doll that had become me—there were so many layers, I wasn't even sure where the real me was.

I had flown thousands of miles back to my hometown only to be alone. Geez. It took me two weeks to get to this point of even thinking of exploring. I pretended that I had no idea what brought me here and what I hoped to accomplish. I had spent so many years with objectives and plans and agendas that the sheer blankness of what was in front of me was more frightening than anything I could imagine. I had read about the astronauts living alone for months in orbit and the sheer vastness of space. There were times and places when the thought of infinity and vastness was pure excitement. Now I was sitting in a room alone while hurtling through space, and I was beyond terrified.

I laughed at my stupidity. It was as though the seconds were circling a race track and the laps were accumulated, and there I was trapped in the middle of the circle watching my defeat.

All this thought and reflection leading nowhere was procrastination. I moved around the bed and toward my suitcase. I found the hidden compartment where I usually kept important documents. I could see the newspaper clipping remained as I had initially received it. The letter sat enticingly next to it.

I studied it like I had studied it every night for the last month—or was it a month and a half? I peered over at the alarm clock next to my bed. The bright red glowing light displayed the time and, with an additional click, the date. The date was now so perilously close to the anniversary date of the article, a June date, eons ago—but not eons enough. Assembling the pieces of the puzzle that brought me here wasn't a task for the faint of heart. Each piece was finely crafted with razor sharp edges. Putting them together would inevitably draw my blood.

I examined the article again front and back, back and front. I could clearly see the name of the paper in the top right corner above the date. *Pauley River Times*. Yep. It was indeed my hometown paper. The letter needed no newspaper byline. In the artificial lighting of the room, it was menacing in its simplicity. Loose-leaf paper and blue ink were enough to terrify me. Years ago, they were my source of happiness. Together these two reminders of my past had lured me back from where I had been safely hiding for years.

My career was over, and I no longer had a choice; it was all about going forward by going backward.

I had to venture outside if I was going to get anywhere, though. The wheel started to spin, and I joined the race. When going in circles, chasing and being chased can look to be the same thing. I knew my landlady could at least recommend a nearby spot to eat. Never once did I expect to awaken on a couch so close to ancient times. Something inside told me there were pleasant memories to be found. I was clueless as to how to search for them. Yet, like a wondrous gift, they remained where I had left them.

CHAPTER 9

Going back to confront Rachel preoccupied my soul the entire night from the moment I returned back to my layer. The extent to which she was the keeper of a great mystery needed to be explored.

Fear circled inside me, waiting to pounce. While I lay in bed, I could picture her soft eyes and motherly smile. *What fangs did lurk behind those lips?* I wondered. *Could she be so cruel as to seem so sincere? Why would she not have said anything when I was with her?* Then again, maybe she knew I would figure it out and eventually return.

There was still a way out. I could go back to California to salvage my old existence and forget about this place again. Yet there was something that drew me here as a salmon would return to its sacred waters to . . . hmm. *Did the salmon return to die or spawn, or both?* The thoughts fluttered around, moths to a devouring flame.

The date on the newspaper stared at me. It was now almost twenty years ago to the day. I pulled the blanket up over my head and tried to sleep in a near fetal position. I looked out the window as the clouds crept in front of the moon. I knew that no matter what, the person I was currently would no longer be the same. *Had I come here to die? Did I cheat death the first time and need to be forgiven of that sin?* I put the newspaper clipping to the side and pulled out the loose-leaf paper. The handwriting, so recognizable, hypnotized me. I held the letter close to my heart as if keeping it warm while I drifted off into a slumber. *If only Avery was here. She would protect me, even if it was only to protect me from myself.* I couldn't ask her, or anyone I cared about, to sacrifice for me. I wondered if maybe I was apprehensive about something far worse than dying.

My night was spent in and out of consciousness. My alarm clock didn't even have to ring to give the new day its birth. The clouds had taken their positions in the sky, sentinels awaiting the marauding sun. They stood at their posts from the previous night, directing the rain that fell steadily. I put on a pair of jeans and the plain plaid shirt I had with the blue and black squares. It was apparel I had out west for cold nights along the beach although rarely worn until recently. An umbrella could protect me from the rain. No way was I going to ring the bell downstairs and ask for one, though. Foregoing the certainty of an interrogation trumped any risk of getting drenched.

I vaguely remembered the address of Rachel's place. It was close enough to where I grew up that I knew how to get back there.

Any fashion sense I possessed became irrelevant as I approached the mirror with an untucked shirt. I looked at my face and could see the shadowy circles hiding beneath the sunken eyes. My beard had grown thicker and made me look sinister and hermit-like in appearance. I unbuttoned the top two buttons of my shirt to expose a vulnerable neck.

I took a razor blade and twiddled it in my hands. I reached for the shaving cream. It splattered into my hands and on my face with the precision of a grenade blast. I took the razor and peeled away at the fur protecting my skin and appearance. Within a minute, my face was fully exposed as the beard disappeared, the tiny hairs drowning in the sink. I watched as they succumbed to the water and slid hopelessly into the drain amidst the gentle snow of the cream. The mirror divulged that same ghostly appearance that probably scared so many women off in the past. Only Avery had been able to accept me valiantly.

My breakfast was handfuls of cornflakes stuffed into my mouth. Now nourished and prepared, I left my building. The bus stop was a five-minute walk down the street. Before I departed, I walked over to the window and opened it for the spider. He could choose either to escape or sit in silence for fresh meat to stray into his trap.

The calendar on my wall was a jumble of letters and numbers, except for one date. The date seemed to stare back at me in sinister fashion. The puzzle pieces grew larger as if taunting me to assemble them, making themselves look so easy to put in place.

I walked along the street to the stop, realizing how unfamiliar I was with this section of the city. Every building seemed the same. Condos stood where low-cost housing used to be.

I chose not to call Avery or Rob. I didn't want them directing me one way or another. Rob's anger probably hadn't completely discharged yet. I waited for the bus, reflecting upon the path I had taken. An audible sigh trickled out of my mouth before my lips could close ranks around it. My fingertips glided across the front of my shirt and made their way to my breast pocket. The letters, ever loyal and patient, waited for their rediscovery. I either had totally overdressed for a potentially warm day or underdressed for the coolness of the river breeze when the sun receded.

With no headphones, book, or any other distractions, I waited for the bus. A girl and her mother sidled up next to me. The girl was in her teens with long, thick black hair and large brown eyes. The mother was slightly younger than me, with curly brown hair and similar brown eyes.

"I hope they'll still have some cute dresses left, eh Mom?" asked the young girl.

"Of course, they will. Don't worry. We'll go to every store if we have to and find you a nice dress to wear," said her mom.

"Thanks, Mom. I'm so excited for the graduation dance," the girl said with eyes opened bright and a smile that lit the dreary day.

"It was sweet of him to ask you. He's a nice boy, right?" she said, smiling at the girl.

"Yes. I like him. I was kind of hoping he would ask, you know," she said, beaming.

The mom looked at me, probably realizing how exuberant their conversation was. "Big night for her. Needs a dress for her dance."

"I'm sure she'll find the perfect one," I said to both of them.

Just then, the bus arrived. I moved slightly to the side to allow them to go in first. I clutched the letter in my hand as

I boarded the bus. I must've looked uncertain because when I got to the driver, he stared at me. "Do you know where you're going, sir? You seem confused. There's another one that takes you out of town. And it comes by every hour."

"Yeah. Sorry. I wasn't sure if this was the right bus. But, now I am. This is the bus I want to take. I'm certain." While I remained confused over where I would end up, my instincts told me this bus would take me there.

He laughed and said, "You can change your mind later. The bus never stops running."

I sighed, fighting back emotions that ran through me, desperate to break out. "It wasn't important." As I walked to the back of the bus and passed the girl, she glanced right up at me and smiled. Although my head was down, I could see her as I went by. I held on tightly to the letter in my hand, almost crumpling it, and looked up with salty, watery eyes and smiled back. She reminded me of the naïve hope I once had. The one I lost.

"Have fun," I said.

The mother smiled at me and said laughingly, "Oh, to be sixteen again, right?"

I bit my lip and nodded, continuing to a secluded spot at the back of the bus.

I sat and stared out the window. It was about a twenty-five-minute ride regularly, yet it seemed to last forever in some ways. I watched as the bus glided in fits and stops past tree-lined residential streets. I could, in the recesses of my ear, start to hear the gentle roar of the river as we approached the other side of town. My mind had played so many tricks on me recently. I was unsure of whether it was my imagination or not.

The bus arrived near the park. I could now see the slow incline of greenery up Shep's Hill and make out the wooded area at the top of the slope leading to the river on the other side. On the far side of the park was my old high school. Without straining my eyes too much, the path I walked upon for years to and from the school came into view. Surrounding all of this was a maze of houses.

I got off the bus at the next stop. My old house was two stops farther down with another five-minute walk. As soon as I periscoped around to check my surroundings, I recognized Rachel's street from the previous day. In my youth, I hadn't spent much time in this district, as it was on the opposite side of the school. The rain had let up when a strong gust of tepid wind emerged. Summer was no longer on the horizon: it had arrived. My now-naked face could nevertheless still feel the coolness of the air coming from the river.

Shep's Hill captured my attention, pulling my stare to the forest behind it. In the distance, I could just see the outline of a box-like enclosure that stood camouflaged inside the woods. After all these years, it remained. Suddenly, the stillness of the image was broken by movement—a ghostly apparition walking through the forest to the front of the shack. I blinked my eyes, and the figure vanished almost as suddenly as it had appeared. There was something familiar about the figure, or perhaps it was my fanciful imagination. But I was no longer surprised by any tricks my mind played to rattle me. Such was life.

I took pride in finding Rachel's bungalow when it came into view around a corner. I wondered if she would even be there at this hour. It wasn't like I had any other place to go—I'd have an eternity to wait for her if she wasn't there. A gentle drizzle started again as I turned onto her street.

I ambled up the walkway, thinking of the girl from the bus. The world to her was alive and singing. Her only worry was finding a dress to wear to a dance. *If only it could stay that way.* Life forever revolved around those moments of happiness when every song felt like its composition existed for you and you alone.

I took a moment to find some reason to turn around and go back west. I knew escaping was no longer an option. There were no "none of the above" options in life either. I took a hefty breath and hoped for the girl to have the simple life of finding the right dress and the right song for her first dance. If only, I thought, I could make it happen. It was past the twilight hour for me but maybe not for someone else. It all seemed frivolous as I stared at the white door with the peeling paint. *Is it silly that I would care for a total stranger?* My mind procrastinated, logic hammering the emotions back into place.

In my delusion, I figured I stared at the door for barely a second, not more than a couple. It was far longer. The wood porch step creaked loudly as I shifted my weight back and forth. The doorbell loomed at eye level to my left, quietly taunting me. Before I could lift my arm, the door slowly opened. I could see green eyes peering uncertainly through the crack of the door.

PART 2: WHEN THE MOON SANG
CHAPTER 10
High School

The first day of any school year always triggered trepidation in my heart. The leaves were about to turn, if they hadn't already, and while still bright when you woke up, you knew the morning darkness approached with the coming of the cold.

Today was a little different. I had just turned fifteen; in two years, I would be in college. My birthday marked the end of the summer season, year in and year out. It was not like I didn't enjoy school or did poorly. I looked forward to seeing the "school friends" or, rather, the kids who seemed to disappear over the course of the summer and reinvented themselves each fall. Most of my summers were spent not venturing too far off the beaten path. Pickup baseball games and swimming at the local park were my activities of choice. A few days out of town with the parents for a brief trip in a good year. The summer always came and went so fast. This was true every year.

Upon awakening, I took an unusually long look at myself in the mirror. My murky brown hair had grown long as the summer progressed, offering a hint of curl at the ends just above my ears. My skin was moderately tanned. I spent much of the afternoons with headphones on and a book in my hand. Gone, mercifully, were the oily patches of skin. I prayed I wouldn't have to live with the acne and, dare I say it, the "boils" of the last two years. I filled my hands with cold water and, as was the ritual every morning, buried my face in them. The frigid water across my eyes revitalized me.

I slipped back into my room to loiter on the edge of my bed. I closed my eyes. I thought about what this year might have in store for me. I had grown a lot taller since the spring; shaving was now a daily necessity. I wondered which teachers I would have and would my innate shyness still provide shelter. I felt this year was going to be different. It scared me a lot, realizing I may no longer be able to simply run and hide.

For the first time this summer, I felt alone for a reason I couldn't figure out. Relatives and friends assumed my loneliness went hand in hand with not having any siblings. Not true. I played a multitude of sports, none with any great physical prowess, but, always good enough to be under the radar of ridicule. When activities finished for the day, I'd be home listening to music or reading. I enjoyed that comfort and solitude until recently. I felt isolated when my friends and other kids went home for the day. I sensed a touch of grief when the numbers dwindled in the park as the kids went on their vacations with their parents. It was a new emotion and something strong enough inside to agitate me. Hours would pass with me sitting with my eyes closed trying to understand.

My parents sensed the change, too, and could see me distancing myself from them. They also knew better than to probe or interrogate.

The new school year suddenly held many opportunities and challenges as well. *What if I still felt isolated and apart? Why do I suddenly need to not be alone?* I smiled and laughed to myself that I had gotten fed up with listening to my thoughts . . . finally, I supposed.

The house was eerily quiet that morning. It was normal to hear my mom with the toaster or a frying pan, making an improvised breakfast to be ready like clockwork by the time I meandered down the stairs to the kitchen. My dad was up and out at the crack of dawn for his long commute to work. I often got up earlier to catch breakfast with him and beat him to the newspaper so I could announce the scores before he got to see them. When he did get to the paper first, I managed to pry away the comic section to get my daily dose of the *Far Side* or *Calvin and Hobbes. If only I could draw.*

I could smell the food from the kitchen. Oatmeal with a cinnamon hint. No other noise. Yes, this was a different day and the dawn of new era. My mom had re-entered the workforce, and she would no longer be home in the mornings when I rose. I was on my own. Naturally, I believed my mom became tired of the same old routine, so when she announced she had a job, I was genuinely pleased. What I overheard later on was my parents talking about how the extra income would be kept aside for the future. My dad, perhaps, had finally started considering retiring one day.

Generally, I would have been elated to have the house to myself for even an hour or so before school. Not anymore. I missed the organized chaos of starting the day with my mom. Although I would barely say a word to her on most mornings, it was the energy of her presence that was comforting.

I found a pair of jeans that were ripped at the knee. I hated new jeans and loved my worn Levis and now no one could give me grief for the grass stains on them. I bore in mind the school rule . . . no shorts or ripped shirts. I threw on a plain striped Rugby shirt, yellow and blue, and hurried down the stairs to eat. I sang to myself, punctuating each verse with a creak of the wood stairs.

While I was sitting alone at the table, my heart slowly began to race. *Who would I sit with at lunch?* I hadn't thought of it before. I would look like the biggest dork sitting by myself in the cafeteria. It would be the first year I would be eating lunch in the cafeteria with the other kids. I always came home for lunch before since I lived so close to school. With mom at work now, it no longer made sense to leave the school for lunch. Suddenly, I would be with three hundred or so other kids at lunch. My heart was beating faster now. I mean, I had enough friends at school, but now I was the newbie at lunch. The thoughts raced through my head like a good stock car race, crashing into each other into a jumbled pile in my mind. All ugly and gross to visualize.

An even worse thought seeped in: *what if I ended up labeled as a geek, nerd, and general outcast?* I played sports and all, but I read and did well in school. I didn't speak much in class, preferring to stay unnoticed. Now all this would come back to torture me. I washed out my bowl and decided to just follow my friend Thomas at noon. Hopefully, we'd be in same class before lunch or have lockers near each other. I may be able to just tag along. Thomas was a neighbor and long ago had determined he was too lazy to come home for lunch. He had the routine down; I was sure of it. If I could just hang out with him, I would be okay. Normally I walked by his house to meet him before school, so I would make certain he would save a spot for me.

The school hadn't changed since junior high school. The same red brick structure. The sun was bright in the sky. As the masses assembled, I still felt apart and a little comfortable. While the eyes of the guys around me were dancing around to see what changes the summer had brought and picking out which girls had entered their top ten lists, the girls were scoping the boys, doing the same.

I sat on the grass near the entrance and exhaled. We were getting older. The school year began as it always did—with the crisp wind and bright September sun. New clothes, new hairstyles. The same first-day fashion shows. The same first-day discussions of what summer was like. It was all the same ritual, except one thing had changed. I was not a little kid anymore and would not be younger tomorrow or the day after. When the bell rang to go in, I raised my hands to my face and felt the stubble from the spots I missed. *Too late now.*

Two more years and then college. I acknowledged the smiles thrown my way with a grin. I wanted to soak it all in. Not sure why at that time, it just felt right. I took a million photos with my mind that morning as we walked inside the building, the paint still smelling fresh from the last-second coat put on to give it that new look again.

The school year began without incident or embarrassment. I had a permanent spot in the cafeteria, thanks to Thomas. There wasn't much time to talk at lunch. I learned pretty quickly how chit-chatting at the table was not tolerated. It was a sit down, open your bag, scoff, and take off operation. We only had fifty minutes, so the smokers ate quickly to step out to get a puff or two. Even kids who didn't smoke took off outside to hang out. Beginning November 1st, we would be in "lockdown" mode, unless going home for lunch, and not allowed outside again until April. I guess the school was worried about kids freezing to death, although smoking just outside the doors was somehow tolerated.

I spent my lunch hour most days finishing my meal at a leisurely pace and then wandering off to the gym to shoot some baskets with a couple of other guys or finding a quiet spot and putting on my headphones. I could smile at the girls walking by and avoid any uncomfortable small talk. There were some pretty girls in the school. I just didn't know how to bridge the gap between us or what to say or how to speak to them without sounding like an idiot. Rather than crash and burn trying, I chose to stay quiet and close to the land, unsure how many knew who I was anyways. It wasn't like I didn't want to go outside with the others. It was just that they ate so fast and left so quickly, I didn't want to be the tail of the dinosaur. Besides, nobody invited me. Not even Thomas. Thomas was a big-time smoker and by 11:30 was climbing the walls for a drag. It would have been awkward to start going outside with the guys, especially now since they would have felt sorry not asking me.

I honestly assumed they didn't think I would be interested.

***

Christmas came and went. Before you knew it, half the school year was over. The winter announced itself with a thick blanket of white during the holidays, the sins of the summer now buried. I had gotten used to my new routine. I had my spot at lunch and quiet time after school.

We all returned the first week of January trudging our way through the knee-deep snow. I got to my locker and dusted the snow off my pant leg and left what would be a huge puddle in front of my locker, which I managed to step in. My feet would be soaked all day. Shit. Double shit. I looked at the clock and realized I still had five minutes to first period, which was history. I could take off my socks and run to the washroom and, hopefully, get them dry fast enough using one of the hand dryers. In bare feet, I raced across the cold concrete floor of our locker bay toward the washrooms by the gym. As I ran into the restroom, I thought I had gone unnoticed.

"Man. If it isn't a prophet himself. Running barefoot through a school! Cool. Is this the dress code?" said a deep gravelly voice.

"Sorry, sir," I said, thinking it was a teacher or a principal of all people. "My socks are wet. I just wanted to dry them."

"Relax, man. Don't sweat it. I'm not going to rat you out," the confident voice said.

I looked back to see who was speaking. To my surprise, it

was a student, a new student. "Sorry. I totally thought you were a teacher . . . I mean, you know."

"Hey, man. Do I look like a teacher? Do I look like a fricken authority figure? You got nothing to be sorry for. I thought anyone running barefoot had to be the second coming. We can use a little of the JC. You know what I mean?" he said, grinning.

"Look, I can't say I know everyone here, and I've been in this town for years. You are new. I don't recall seeing you in the fall." I was never great at eye contact, so I didn't see his reaction initially.

He was slightly taller than me with broad, athletic shoulders. He had long sandy brown hair almost to his shoulders and a hint of a beard. He was my age, yet seemed older in many ways. He had a cross around his neck, a black T-shirt under a very faded jean jacket, and had jeans even more worn than I did, and wore construction boots. What did catch my eye was the union jack logo on one front pocket of his jacket and an unmistakable logo on the other. Blue and white circles, wrapped around a red bull's eye.

"Yeah, I am new. Went to St. Peter's Academy until Christmas. Now I'm here. And the first guy I meet is straight out of the bible. That blows me away," he said teasingly.

"You like The Who?" I asked, gesturing to the lapel of his jacket.

"Man, for some prophet, there is a lot you don't know. No one puts a band's logo on their damn clothes unless they are a true worshipper of the rock altar they play on."

"Of course, silly me." Just then the first bell rang, and

I prepared to sprint off when his hand grabbed my arm forcefully.

"What's up with the running? No performer ever goes on stage on time. Let the audience wait. The show will be well worth it." He winked at me and for some bizarre reason, I was in on whatever act he was performing.

"Right." Suddenly I was walking at a pace slower than maple syrup in March. My socks were left on top of the dryer, and by the time I reached history class, it was too late. As I walked into Room 176, I could hear the whispers, "Where are his shoes?" With the new kid behind me, I had no way to go but forward.

The voice behind me said, "I'll sit in the back of the class. You sit next to me in case I need answers. I know you'll have the answers."

I grabbed a seat at the back, and sure enough, my new friend took the one right next to me. I think half the class was looking at my bare feet, and the other half was looking at the new kid. I was getting my notepad and pen out of my bag when I noticed a figure hovering over me.

"Mr. Wells, it seems that you have forgotten your foot apparel today. What will it be tomorrow: no shirt, no under-wear, or will you be going total Roman on us and be wearing a toga?" said the voice in a stern whisper.

"Sorry, Mrs. Lewiston. My socks got wet, and I went to dry them, and the bell went off. I forgot about them. It won't happen again."

"I am sure it won't. Please leave and get your shoes and socks right away."

"Thanks."

"I'll go with him since he probably forgot where he left them and to make sure he comes back in one piece," said the stranger, leaping out of his chair and hurrying across the classroom amid the laughter that now had started.

I turned back quickly to the see the new kid following me. Behind him, I could see the smiling class, and the biggest surprise was the smile on Mrs. Lewiston's face. She was clearly enjoying the distraction on the first day of the winter semester.

I waited for the new kid to catch up with me. "You know that is the first time I have seen Mrs. Lewiston smile—and probably the first time she has spoken to me and I cannot believe I didn't get a detention."

"You must be kidding. She likes you. You must be an excellent student. I can tell. Besides teachers can have a sense of humor. They all do."

"I'm serious. I had her last semester. I didn't even think she knew my name."

"She is a cutie. Maybe a bit too old for you. I'll fix you up with someone your age who isn't married. You got my word."

"What makes you think I need to be fixed up?" I wasn't very convincing in my bare feet, torn jeans, and wearing a shirt only a mom would buy for her son.

"Okay, okay. You can do your own fishing, just do not catch what I throw back. I'm sure you know that looks bad."

"Deal. By the way, what's your name and what are you doing here, besides getting me expelled?"

"Name is Marius. You do not need to know my last name.

First-name basis, since I saved you from history class. We're blood brothers now. I should let you know I was kicked out of my last school."

"No way."

"Between you and me, the story is that I got kicked out. The truth is my dad lost his job and couldn't afford it anymore, so here I am." Suddenly, his face took on a serious expression. There was no doubt he was entrusting me with the truth.

"Hey, nothing wrong with that. Trust me. You won't have any trouble making anyone believe you got kicked out. No offense."

"None taken. By the way, it would be a good idea if your socks weren't inside out."

I think it took a few minutes to walk back to class. I sheepishly entered the class with my head down. With my seat all the way at the back, I knew I would have to run the gauntlet of leering faces. Fortunately, as I made my way in, I could hear Marius's voice boom.

"Mrs. Lewiston, allow me to introduce myself. My name is Marius. I'm the new kid. I humbly apologize for disrupting what might be the very best lecture in the school. It won't happen again."

By then, I had reached my seat and all eyes were transfixed on the stranger. I was safe and had flown under the radar until . . .

"I do apologize, Mrs. Lewiston and classmates, for mistaking my dear friend for the Savior. It was the bare feet that threw me off!"

I could just form a faint smile as the classroom roared with laughter. I fixed my eyes on my desk until it was over, barely feeling Marius as he messed my hair before he sat down. When I finally mustered the courage to look up at Mrs. Lewiston, she shook her head with a broad smile on her face and went back to her lesson.

As in all schools, news of a new student got around fast, in this case, by lunchtime, it was the talk of the grade. By second period, Thomas had found me in the hallways.

"I heard what happened. Were you the kid with the bare feet? Seriously?"

"Yes."

"Cool. That is chick-magnet material. Good stuff. I'll have your spot saved for lunch. See you then."

At that moment, I knew that finding a quiet place by myself to chill was not going to happen. I also felt a lot less isolated than I had in months.

The arrival of Marius in my second to last year of high school—and my life—is most easily described simply as welcome. He forced me to stay in tune with his lead or be exposed and spotlighted as a helpless outsider. I played rhythm guitar behind his vocals. He was loud at the worst of times and, thankfully, incredibly confident and self-aware at the best. In his way, he gave me a voice I never knew I had. He often repeated observations that I whispered to him in class and plated them like a skilled chef to his captive audience, student, and teacher alike. I found it intriguing to see my words trigger such delight. I was the composer, and he was the singer.

Marius was not the model student by anyone's stretch of imagination. It was evident his spare time was spent just being cool. Alternatively, he had every seventies rock song memorized. He could easily recite the lyrics when pressed. Granted, each song carried the same melody when sung by him. No one dared call him out on it.

He was physically imposing at almost six feet tall. His jacket pocket usually had a pack of Marlboros partially exposed.

I couldn't understand the interest Marius had in me or why he took me under his wing. At the best of times, I was a flawed anti-hero in his great epic. Feeling awkward with my head lowered as girls passed, I avoided any semblance of eye contact at all costs. Despite my shyness, he chose me as his friend from that first day we met. He would seek me out when he got a test result or needed help. When bored, he would focus the attention on me, knowing how uncomfortable that would make me. There were times when I thought he looked down on me as the squeaky toy for a playful dog. However, he would always apologize after for putting me on the spot and then tell me just to relax and enjoy. "Kiran," he would say, "there are plenty of days ahead to be old and boring. Just not on my watch." The one thing that was clear was that I considered him my friend and deep down I knew he had my back.

There was jealousy over having this new character soaking up the limelight and being popular with the girls at school. Because of it, the others in my grade who I sort of hung around with, like Thomas, kept a distance from Marius, and therefore, from me. I suspected that they no longer knew how I fit into our circle of friends and, more specifically, how I no longer fit into the cell they had kept me in all these years.

The winter semester passed quickly, my grades improved with my newfound confidence, and spring was soon approaching. A rumor spread around our class of a new student joining us shortly. Apparently, someone was transferring from another school. The term "bullied" came up in conversation. He supposedly skipped a grade years earlier.

As we were leaving the school one day, I mentioned to Marius that I heard a new student was coming. He grinned at me and said, "Don't worry. I already know. Mrs. Lewiston told me to be on 'exemplary' behavior with him, or else."

"I heard he's younger."

"Yeah. I heard a year or so. I guess they don't want me corrupting him, too." He laughed.

"Really, who else did you corrupt?" I laughed at my question. "Ah, I see."

CHAPTER 11

The morning bell rang, and everyone lined up to go back inside when I felt a tug on my sleeve. It was now early March, and it had been an unusually warm beginning to the last month of winter. We'd gotten to school early to play touch football. With each passing day, the arrival of a new student grew less likely.

"Hey, Wells! I think you left your jacket on the fence."

"Shit. You're right, thanks." I looked across to the far end of the schoolyard. Sure enough, my jacket was hanging on the steel fence where I'd hung. I could also see a solitary figure moving toward it. I knew I was going to be late, but the darn jacket was new. There was no way I was going to let anyone steal it. "Who's the kid near the fence?"

"No idea. Must be someone's younger brother."

Marius looked up and guessed. "New kid. I can smell the young blood a mile away."

"Weird that he's coming to us so late in the year."

"I heard he moved in with his aunt. Some crazy stuff with his parents."

The rumors swirled like a Sahara sandstorm, as they always did with a new student. Stories in high school went viral quickly. They took root, whether they were true or not. It was rare for someone to change school this late in the year. Usually, it was beginning of a semester. His must be a special case.

What a way to start a day. I raced across the yard as fast as I could, not taking my eyes off the jacket or the guy hovering around it. The funny thing was that as I got closer, I realized he wasn't even trying to steal it. He was just standing and walking in a semi-circle around it, almost like he was studying it. I stopped about six to eight feet behind him. His back was turned. I could have clocked him, and he would never have seen it coming.

Silently, I inched forward and was sure he must have heard my footsteps or my heavy breath. He didn't budge. He continued to move from side to side.

I glanced at him from head to toe when I noticed it. He had a royal blue spring windbreaker on. I could barely tell if he had shoes on. Looked like he was wearing a long black thing like a dress beneath his jacket. *Oh, great! A freak. A real freak.* Now I started worrying about being alone out here with him.

"Nice jacket," a soft voice quietly said. So quiet that I could barely hear. "What kind is it?"

"Umm but, like, no offense. Who are you? I got to get going. I'm already late for class." I reached up and took the jacket off the fence and put it on.

"I guess I'm late, too. I'll follow you, then, so I know where to go."

"I've never seen you before."

He looked at me, almost laughing, and then turned to face the school. His eyes grew small as he peered at the building. He turned to me with a silly look in his eyes. "I'm new. I guess I got caught daydreaming. Gets me in trouble all the time. My aunt warned me about that."

"You're the newbie, I guess."

"No, I've been around a long time. Probably as long as you. Just because you don't know me doesn't make me new."

"Don't be a smartass. You know what I meant. Where are you from, besides outer space?"

He started laughing. "You're not the first to say that. Outer space. That is kind of funny, actually. Like, maybe the moon. Only I'm not that old. Still, it is a nice jacket."

"Yes, it is, thanks. I got it this summer. It's a war jacket. Kind of like the ones they wore in World War Two."

"You mean a fighter pilot jacket. I read a lot about them. It's almost exactly like an RAF fighter jacket. It even has a sheep wool collar. It's cool. Is it your dad's or grandad's?"

"No. They didn't fight in that war. I bought it this summer. It's not real." I slowly started walking back to school as I was speaking, as if to lead him there. I had a feeling he would have stayed near the fence all morning otherwise. "Truth is, it isn't the jacket I really wanted. I just couldn't afford the other one. What's your story?"

"My aunt and I just moved here from out west. We lived near the desert. Never saw snow before. I'm so excited for next winter. I live with my aunt, always have."

"Snow you will see. Don't worry about that. I live a couple of blocks that way," I said, pointing past the fields beyond the fence. "I cut across those fields to get to school each day."

"Great. I live not too far, Willow Ridge Road."

This character lived a few blocks from me. Luckily, he lived on the opposite side of the park. Now that I told him of the shortcut through the fields, he might follow me home one day. I started shaking my head.

"You seem to be worried. Maybe it's your first day? Are you nervous, too?"

I caught myself enjoying the discussion and started to laugh. "Don't be nervous. I'm not—just worried 'cause we're late, that's all. It's a good school and most of the kids are cool."

I stopped walking at that point as my curiosity got the better of me. "What are you wearing under your jacket? I sincerely hope that is not a dress."

He started laughing. "Why would you think it's a dress? Just because it's long. No. It is, without a doubt, a Jesuit robe."

"Seriously. Is that not like a priest thing; how would you get one?"

"Been in my family for years. One of my ancestors was a priest who came over from Europe and settled here. Came to convert people. When I moved here, my grandma gave it to me as a gift. I guess one of my ancestors didn't like the cold and moved where it was warm, and left it behind."

"Wow. You know it's not as bad as I thought. That's a pretty cool story, but, like, aren't you scared of ruining it or losing it? Like, shouldn't it be in a museum?"

He look at me, puzzled. "You know my aunt said the same thing when my grandma pulled it out. My grandma said it probably was good luck to whoever wore it back then, especially coming to the New World, and it would be a waste not to wear it, especially since it's pretty warm."

"What about your parents?"

"My dad disappeared when I was young; my mom was too young to raise me on her own."

"Sorry. I didn't mean to pry like that."

"Don't be sad." He could see the worried look in my eyes. "Be happy. My aunt adopted me." But even though he smiled at me, I could detect some melancholy in his voice.

As I looked at his face, I could see clear blue eyes shining innocently below the long black bangs of his hair. His nose was small and pointed. He looked no more than thirteen or fourteen. He turned his head briefly at the chirp of a robin building her nest nearby, and I could see a greenish mark on his cheek. A bruise. One that was slowly fading away and surely the size of a fist.

"Who hit you?" I pointed to his cheek, almost close enough to touch it.

"This little bruise? I had a disagreement with someone at my old school, and, well, he was not happy with me."

"Not happy with you…He punched you. He obviously hit you."

"I guess you could say that. I didn't want to get him in trouble because sometimes I say things I shouldn't and people get mad at me." He shook his head dejectedly as if admitting some great personal failure.

"Whatever could you have said to make someone hit you? It's not like you're much of a physical threat. No offense."

"He was talking about something in science class. I tried to set him straight."

"Really. Do continue."

"Well, I told him that everything is in our minds and that dreams are real. They do happen. Just in another place. There are millions of these other places, by the way."

"Again, really," I said half-laughingly yet, somehow genuinely interested. "I don't get why he would punch you for saying that."

"He called me weird and said I dressed like a girl." His voice got low as his eyes began blinking rapidly.

"Sorry, I didn't mean to offend you about your clothes. But I don't think you can wear your cloak, so to speak, to class, though."

"Did you think I would wear this to class? No, I'll take it off as soon as I have my locker. I just like it because it belonged to someone who lived long before me. Also, it tends to break the ice," he said, smiling. I could see his hand pop out from under the robe and make its way through the sleeve of his windbreaker. "I'm Andrew. Nice to meet you."

"My name is Kiran, and it is nice to meet you—even if we are ten minutes late on your first day."

"Now you have to show me where I have to go next."

***

At lunchtime, I could see this new kid circle the cafeteria with his food tray, not knowing where to sit. However, he didn't seem to care.

He was in one of my classes. The teacher had a helluva time even getting to his last name as Andrew interrupted her with a long history of his fourteen-year life and how much he looked forward to teaching us all. Correction, he promised *not* to teach us. Originally, it was what I thought I heard. When I thought about it, I realized he said something different. I should make a particular point of that. He promised to "awaken us."

I sat in what was now my customary spot, usually at the end of the long table against the wall and directly across from Marius. The place was partially hidden from view, which is why he liked it so much. Sometimes he actually smoked in the cafeteria, the only kid who would dare do that in the building. I could see the new kid having a hard time making a decision. He looked like a bird whose wing was clipped and not so much looking where to land as to crash.

"Andy! Andy! There's a spot over here next to me."

Marius looked up at me, obviously surprised at my tone. He looked back over his shoulder and saw Andrew.

"Spaceman priest. You're inviting him to eat with us. I heard the guy was wearing a dress this morning."

"Not a dress. A cloak. Like the one a spiritual missionary wore. A shaman. Kind of like a Jim Morrison type." I was making it up as I went along.

Marius was grinning at me and rolling his eyes at same time.

"Seriously. The kid has no friends. He totally is all right." I had to get Marius's buy-in fast. "He worships the moon. He's into some cult stuff, I think." It was as egregious a lie as I had ever spoken. I knew it was Marius, of course, so in his world, this could be the truth, for all I knew.

Marius's look of utter disbelief at the sight of this eccentric child was indescribable. I could see him studying Andy, presumably looking for weakness. I watched his eyes move from foot to head, and head to foot again. It was almost as though a flash went off and Marius's eyes focused in on Andy's face and honed in on his cheeks. It was the bruise. The faded evidence of violence.

Now I could see Marius's facial expression change. Nothing intrigued Marius more than someone who was off the wall. His expression was much deeper than intrigue. I could see his lips purse at the sight of tarnished cheek and his eyes blinked in a sympathetic symphony of movement. He was clearly unnerved and quickly caught himself when he noticed my stare out of the corner of his eye.

"He's a moon worshipper?"

"Yes. He loves the night, kind of like a . . ."

"Don't say vampire. Now I know you're putting me on."

I started to chuckle and then got serious as Marius's face grimaced at my attempt to gain favor for a stranger. "C'mon. He doesn't know anyone here. You owe me for last chemistry test."

"Frick. You keep bringing that up. You got an eighty-nine percent, not a hundred. I could hardly see half your answers. Stop wearing those fucking high-collared shirts."

"You owe me!"

"All right." I could tell, though, he was not going to let this go easily.

Thomas and Dale came over and tried to take their spots next to us. Marius put out his hand like a stop sign for Thomas.

"What the fuck? Let me sit. I'm starving."

Marius looked up and stared at Thomas. "I'm saving a seat for my new friend."

Thomas looked next to him and could see Andy standing to wait for him to move so he could sit.

"You're serious."

Marius got up and grabbed Andy hard around the collar and pulled him into the seat. He then looked at the rest of the table and put one foot up on his seat.

"Everyone, say hello to my new friend, Moony."

The cafeteria table looked in horror as Andy half stumbled off his chair, trying to decipher who "Moony" was. I quickly leaned over to him and told him his new name was "Moony." Andy looked up at me with his big blue eyes and a wide grin extending from ear to ear. "I like the moon. From now on, I am Moony!" he declared.

Marius slapped down hard on Moony's back with an open hand. "Well, Moony. How has your day gone so far? It's been awhile since we last spoke."

Moony sat there clueless. As far as I knew, they had never met. He now had something that was worth gold. He was in with Marius. Thomas and Dale had seen their spots in the pecking order drop dramatically.

Marius looked over at me while plunging a giant sandwich into his mouth. He raised his finger at me. "No more high-collared shirts on exam days. I can't see over them. Last warning."

CHAPTER 12

Pauley High School underwent a substantial transformation in the early days of April. The snow had fully melted, the blooming of flowers along the slopes of Shep's Hill and the sound of birds building nests all around heralded the beginning of a new cycle. From our classroom, we could hear the roar of the Pauley River finally flowing unencumbered for the first time in months. For us students, it meant two things: The school year was nearing a conclusion, and we were now allowed to leave the school building and go outside at lunch. This edict caused great delight to the smokers. Such was their world.

Meanwhile, Moony's presence in school, while lacking the volatility of Marius's, had a subtle impact. Moony quickly became the school's endangered species, but also came under Marius's protection. Marius took him under his broad, sheltering wings. It was Marius who, during Moony's first week in school, conscripted a fellow student to sew onto Moony's cloak a patch, shaped like the moon.

Moony earned his patch during his first month with us. His interrupting of teachers to clarify their points, his monologues about world issues totally outside of the context of the class lesson, and his "Moony vision," as we called it, were entertaining. Moony, in particular, was the superstar of our comparative religion class. Moony believed that everything in life was an illusion and that we all existed in each other's minds. Our reality, as he described it, was the result of the intersection of the waves of each person's consciousness. There was no difference between dreaming and being awake. It was all one in the same. Perhaps no student in the history of Pauley High School had been so equally reviled in both science and religion classes. His fellow students, myself included, took great delight in the mental gymnastics we watched our teachers perform trying to put out the fires Moony naively set to their lesson plans. If the chaos of Moony wasn't enough, a magnifier was omnipresent. Marius would often raise his hand shortly after a Moony lesson to say, "Sir. Can Andy please repeat what he just said, as I didn't quite understand it the first time?" Perhaps I didn't realize it at the time; Moony may have been the finest performance artist I ever met.

Seniors would pass by my locker to ask me about Moony. Was he a prodigy? Was he a Russian KGB agent? Was he secretly a fifty-year-old NASA scientist? Was he a prophet? Some of these questions were asked only partially jokingly. Moony was just Moony. A fourteen-year-old with an insatiable curiosity and childlike wonder of the world. I rarely grew tired of his wandering thoughts.

We were within the realm of the locker bay area when the announcement came that we would be allowed to go outside for lunch that day. Marius sighed as he surveyed the clock. He wouldn't have to sneak a smoke in the boys' bathroom. We congregated at lunchtime, sitting in our accustomed spots amongst the rows and rows of cafeteria tables. Most ate fast and took off for the outdoors. I sat still, Moony next to me awaiting my cue, as the rest of the table got up to go outside. Marius started walking ahead with Thomas and the rest of the gang close behind when he noticed Moony and me staying put. He told the rest of the group to go out ahead of him.

"C'mon guys. You can yap outside all you want. Let's go!" He declared it in his field general voice. I looked at Marius plaintively with a hint of wistfulness, hoping he would move on without further intimidation. No such luck. What Marius didn't understand was that I was still an outsider to the majority of the group. They didn't invite me, and to them, I was still a geek who didn't smoke or drink. I was still the kid in the dorky shirts his mom picked out. My oversized fighter jacket and my friendship with Marius were my saving grace.

"No. Seriously, Marius. Go on without us. We'll stay and shoot some baskets or get some homework done in the library." The minute the last syllable came out, I could see the color rush to Marius's cheeks. Moony clearly saw it as well, since he slowly pushed back in his chair, trying to make himself invisible.

"The fucking library. You cannot be serious. We can go out now and have some fun at lunch. Do your studying at home on your time!"

"Thanks, Marius. I just don't think they want me around them. They know I don't smoke, and you know they talk about girls." I was now whispering and forced Marius to lean forward to hear. "I don't have any experience with girls.

I don't want them teasing me."

"Scared to be teased?! I tease you all the time."

"That's different. I know you don't mean it. I'd just be standing there like a plant."

Marius stopped short of his next words and was clearly thinking. "I see your point. Listen, do you have a ghetto blaster, a radio with a tape deck at home?"

"Yeah, I do. A good one, too."

"Bring it tomorrow. None of these clowns have one that they can bring. We need to have some music outside."

"Okay," I said nervously. "You'll bring some tapes?" I asked.

"I have the usual stuff: The Who, Zappa, Zeppelin, The Doors, The Clash." He went through his mental list and then looked at me with a grin. "I'm not bringing any of that, though. You bring what you listen to."

"What I have at home is different."

"So long as it's not Liberace, we're good. Is it rock?"

"Yeah. It's new stuff, though. I'm not sure those guys will like it."

"You like it, though?"

"Yes. I listen to it all the time."

"So bring it and stop being difficult. I'll go out and tell them that, beginning tomorrow, you are the musical director. They'll have cool music outside. Everyone will be happy."

"Okay, I suppose." My words slowly slithered back down my throat. It quickly became apparent I made a massive commitment.

"Great." He quickly turned and raced outside, an unlit cigarette already dangling from his mouth.

Moony leaned over to me. "Am I allowed outside with you guys tomorrow?"

"For sure, Moony," I said, clearly distracted by the task at hand. Moony picked up on my discomfort immediately.

"Why are you so nervous? Are you not allowed to bring your radio to school?"

"No, Moony. I can bring the radio. I'm just not sure they'll like the music I bring. These guys are all into that sixties and seventies rock stuff."

"So, it is the eighties. I'm sure they'll still listen to it."

"It's just not stuff you hear on the commercial radio stations. I tape a lot off an obscure radio station I sometimes like to listen to. Kind of on the far left of the dial."

"Something different is always worth hearing. I am honestly looking forward now to tomorrow." He sat back in his chair, almost flipping himself onto his posterior.

"Great, Moony. If it goes haywire tomorrow, just do me a favor and pretend to have an asthma attack."

"I'll practice tonight," he said as he made an exaggerated coughing sound as if practicing.

I shook my head—he was such a character sometimes. "I was just kidding. Let's go hit the library."

As Moony walked ahead of me as we left the cafeteria, I put my hand on his shoulders. "Moony, I'm glad you came to our school."

"Me, too. Wow. Music at lunchtime. Maybe there'll be dancing, too."

"Maybe, Moony. Maybe one day there will be dancing."

CHAPTER 13

The next day, there was a certain air of anticipation. As everyone finished eating lunch, I excused myself to go to my locker to get my radio and the tapes. Moony looked around, not sure who he should follow. Marius finally put him out of his misery. "Moony, come on out with us." It was less of an invite than a demand. Walking away, I could hear the murmurs of displeasure. Some of the kids just tolerated Moony because he was friends with Marius and me. Tolerate was the operative word. I knew that if Moony started singing outside or, worse, dancing to the music, Marius would be there to keep him in his place. I hoped.

I walked down the long corridor to the back exit of the school and into the yard at the rear. I arrived at the back fence and set down my radio. I adjusted the knobs, including volume control to ensure that when I pressed the "play" button an eardrum-shattering noise did not come out and either ruin the speakers or, worse, set off the wave of protests as to why I was even there in the first place.

Dale hovered over me, watching my every twitch. He was tall and very lanky, with a long, crooked nose and an acne-laced complexion. He had curly blonde hair with a hint of a mustache. He thought of himself as a music guru. He claimed he played electric guitar in a band with college kids.

He also liked to talk about all the weed he had access to on the weekends when he would "jam" with his older friends. He was fidgeting with his belt with "ZEP" carved into the buckle. He leaned over me and announced loudly, "Need help? Are you sure you know what you're doing?"

I was reaching into my backpack when the words stabbed into my spine, freezing me. I shook my head and looked back at him, rolling my eyes. "Just give me a sec." I pulled out a tape, one that I listened to religiously. I fumbled with it in my hands. I looked across the schoolyard and could see my circle of friends surrounding me, eyes staring intently. Marius stood at the periphery next to Moony, who was awash with great anticipation. Just outside of the circle and against the steel fence were a bunch of girls in our grade chit-chatting. They were certainly very preoccupied now with the events unfolding in our boys' world. Most of the girls had brightly colored hair, spiky, with piercings on earlobes or around the outer ear. Such was the punk, post-punk girl gang. I could see Janie standing in the middle of them, staring right at me. Her brows perked up and arched as if somewhat surprised to see me as the centerpiece of this commotion.

Janie was one of the first girls I had ever met in my life who was not family. We had been in first grade together and sat near each other. She was a cute six-year-old back then with an attitude foreshadowing the blossoming into an older, more cynical teenager. In the good old days of my crayon-coloring youth, she had the longest, thickest, and most beautiful golden hair I had ever seen. One morning, my short attention span got the better of me. I sat behind Janie as I did each and every day. That day she had a light blue ribbon in her hair, set just at the back. It was picture day, and her mom had apparently taken quite a bit of time to fine tune what I thought was already perfect hair. We were practicing our alphabet and writing it out in pencil. I could see her focused in front of me while I daydreamed. Her blue ribbon got my attention. My eyes became hypnotized with the dance the ribbon did as her head shifted. This blue boat sailing on a sea of endless fine yellow wheat. My eyes narrowed and, in my dreamlike state, I lost control of my right hand. It too got caught in this dance before me and reached out for the blue boat.

Before I could stop it, my hand was wallowing in the softest hair I have ever felt. Suddenly, the calm of my dream was broken by Janie's shriek. It was the first time I had ever heard a swear word out of a girl's mouth.

The class erupted with laughter. The teacher came rushing over to find me looking up at her, innocence in my eyes, right hand still caressing Janie's hair. Had not the teacher arrived at my desk, my hand would have been forever entangled in Janie's hair although likely separated from my body. My punishment was a lengthy note about my behavioral issues to my parents plus a week of after-school sanctions.

My father had a long sit-down with his six-year-old son that evening and explained how boys must be gentlemen and should not touch little girls or play with their hair without their permission. He ordered me to apologize to Janie immediately. I set about to carry out what I knew would be the worst part of my punishment the next day.

I walked up to Janie outside the classroom to offer my sincere regret for my behavior. I cannot recall how many words she heard. I also cannot recall how many feet I recoiled. I do remember that the bruising around my eye took almost two weeks to go away after. It was my first black eye, and I wore it as a badge of misguided courage.

Somewhere along the way, Janie's hair was cut short and the pretty dresses she wore were replaced by jeans, leather jackets, and piercings. I overheard my parents mentioning a couple of years back how Janie's parents had separated. Her father had lost his job and starting drinking until finally he was kicked out of his home. All I can remember is Janie arrived at school one day with her head practically shaved. The day I saw the beautiful blonde hair was gone, I felt a sharp pain in my eye, strange as it may seem. Now I looked across the schoolyard, and she, too, was taking a keen interest in my activity.

The midday spring sun was exceedingly bright and partially blinded me as I was about to put the cassette into the tape deck. I was briefly blinded and dropped the chosen cassette onto the ground. I quickly picked it up, inserted it, and pressed play. The clangy guitar intro coursed from my ears through my heart and feet. It was so familiar and welcoming. Then the raspy voice enthusiastically asked the question which opened "I Will Dare".

The small circle was filled with looks of confusion battered in layers of exaggerated indignity.

"What crap is this?"

"Is this is a joke?"

"Please, someone shut it off and put on the radio instead."

I took a step back dejectedly and lowered my head, focusing on the movement of the ants beneath my feet. Marius attempted to calm the masses, only to be overmatched. Moony stood tapping his feet, enjoying the music. Dale finally emerged from the raucous crowd and stopped in front of me to get control of my radio.

Dale was about to reach down to press the "Stop" button when suddenly a solitary figure strode in front of him and pushed him back. It was Janie.

"What is your problem, Dale? The Replacements are awesome and so is this song. I WANT TO HEAR THE REST!"

Dale was stunned. "I never heard of . . ."

Janie interrupted, in full assault mode. "I know you never heard of them because you still think it's the sixties. Get into my generation, Dale, or try visiting us from time to time."

Dale retreated, mortified and mumbling under his breath. He walked by me, shaking his head as if his sky had fallen. Janie walked over to me and playfully shoved my left shoulder.

"Kiran, can I borrow this tape after lunch and bring it home? I'll give it back to you tomorrow."

"Sure, Janie. No problem. Give it back to me anytime."

"Thanks." She studied me carefully and then said, "I didn't know you were into this type of music. I mean. No offense. I just never pictured you...."

"It's all good, Janie. I listen to this all the time. I like the lyrics."

She smiled at me. "Me, too. If you have more, bring them in and maybe we can trade.

"Sure. No problem."

Before she turned away, she smiled at me. "Your eye healed pretty well I see."

I laughed and looked at her head and longed for that moment when that soft blonde hair would emerge from the short, cropped garden of her head.

I turned to face what had gone from a lynch mob in the making to a collection of dumbfounded teenagers dealing with the realization that the statues of their gods lay toppled at the feet of a girl. Marius stood with a broad smirk on his face. He walked toward me and said, "I knew you could pull it off. Never a doubt." He stated as a devilish grin formed.

Thomas, who had been quiet up until this point, finally spoke up. "Kiran, can you bring the radio tomorrow, too?"

Such is how I became the musical director for the remainder of that school year. It was also the beginning of an endless sequence of Janie borrowing my tapes evolving into CDs later on. She would always start with asking me for a smoke at lunch, knowing full well that I didn't have one. It was her lead into asking to borrow music from me.

Moony stood and listened to music. Shuffling his feet when no one was watching. I always was. Now and then, Moony would ask the now-rhetorical question: Why didn't we ever dance if we had all this great music?

CHAPTER 14

My ascendency to the throne resulted from a bloodless rebellion. It was indeed an unusual spring for me. My music dominated the schoolyard. Rather, it dominated within the kingdom of Marius. Within the few months that Marius had been at Pauley High, he was clearly the undisputed leader of our grade. When school commenced again in the fall, we would be in our final year of high school. I would be one of the ruling elite within the school. Time changes dramatically in your teens. One year held the equivalent of stars forming and dying in the universe. Dramatic changes happened that quickly.

Marius, however, was not a strong student. When asked to read aloud in class, he often stumbled and retreated from the task, hiding behind the mask of humor. I spent enough time with him to see the frustration and cracks beneath the carefully constructed façade. It was after school one day when Marius shed some light on the shadow appearing to creep over him.

"Listen, Wells. I need to ask you something."

"Sure. Can it wait until tomorrow? I need to get home and start studying for our finals."

"That's just it. These finals are important, if I heard correctly."

"Well. Yeah, for sure." I was shocked that he didn't

understand how important, and I knew my tone didn't hide it. "Marius, these finals will affect our college applications. These grades and the ones in the fall."

"I get that. I figured I wouldn't get in on good looks alone."

"What are you worried about? Riverside College usually will accept you if your overall average is over seventy-five percent. It's only those pricey schools in the south that require higher."

"See, I'm worrying because well . . ."

"Don't tell me."

"You're going to Riverside?"

"Like, where else?"

"You have excellent grades, though."

"I do okay. Those other schools require some serious coin." I could sense Marius waiting for me to figure it out. "So, you're worried about your marks?"

"Bingo! I knew you were smart like a wizard first time we met."

"Marius, you called me the Savior. Not the wizard. Moony may be a wizard, not me."

"Right. Just making sure you're paying attention."

"If you're worried, I'll help you study. Come on over to my house anytime."

"Sure, that's a grand idea. I saw the look your parents gave me last time. They would have burned me at the stake if they could get enough firewood."

"Next time, don't swing by with a pack of smokes sticking out of your pocket."

"You promise to help?"

"For sure, just . . ." I served up the perfect volley he so confidently awaited. The spike was coming in loud and hard at my face.

"Great. Just move your arms a bit when I jab you with my pencil. You tend to crouch down too low over your paper when we have an exam. You make it hard to see." He smiled from ear to ear. In typical Marius fashion, he had solved his problem while deftly creating one for myself.

"Oh, crap. Just don't expect me to write the answers on the erasers you throw on my desk. If I get caught, my parents will kill me."

"Don't worry. I would explain to them why their son's grand career went down the toilet bowl. I'm good at explaining things to parents." His face was etched in pure stone right then. No hint of humor or mirth. Suddenly, he burst out roaring with laughter. "Sucker. I had you going. If we get caught, no way am I coming near your house."

***

The final exams came and went. In Marius's world, this called for special celebrations. Marius asked me to meet him at the park the night after the last exam. He would bring a beer for each of us, and we would have a drink in tribute to the end of the school year. I walked home with great fear and terror in my heart. Up until that night, not even an ounce of alcohol had ever passed my lips.

I arrived at the top of Shep's Hill just overlooking the residential community. The sun had long since gone down.

Alone, I sat in almost total darkness. I imagined myself drinking a can of beer and losing control and rolling down the hill like a bowling ball down a greased lane. It would be my certain demise. My first beer followed by my careening down the hill headfirst into the brick wall of the school. The school custodian would call my parents and explain how I was dead and managed to damage school property. A bill would surely be forthcoming.

I stared at the stars and the sky. I never realized how elegant this world truly was. For an instant, the stars and planets in the sky appeared to all belong to me. They glistened as if in chorus with one another. The moon seemed to be an appreciating audience whose view occasionally became obstructed by a marauding, uncultured cloud.

I could hear the rustling of birds in the trees and the soft voices of nature. A mosquito buzzed my ear. I splattered it across my cheek. Its blood mixed with mine on my face. I spat on my hand to wipe it off. Now that the buzz was gone, it was suddenly quiet again. I framed this picture within the walls of my mind. Therein lies the joke and therein was the punchline. There was no one with me to share this moment. My one companion, I splattered across my cheek.

A feeling of nausea bubbled to the surface. I closed my eyes as if to take a picture of what was before me and committed it to my memory. The serene beauty of my vision would be a gift I hoped to save—to share one day.

When I opened my eyes, I saw a tiny figure at the base of the hill. The long flowing robe and awkwardness of the movements left no doubt about who it was. I sat up and peered down at him with great interest. I wanted to run down the hill and ask what he was doing. Instead, I chose to enjoy the show from my VIP seat. It was Moony, in all his magical glory.

Moony was by himself, although his actions suggested a partner, more privy to the chaos of his movements. His feet shuffled as his body bent low. His feet left the ground, the gravity of his cloak holding him down. *My god*, I thought. The kid was trying to leap up and down to catch something. From where I sat on top of the hill, I couldn't see if he was trying to grab a butterfly or maybe only swat away an annoying bug. There was a strange way to his movements, suggesting a dance to music he alone was hearing.

Heavy footsteps behind me announced Marius's arrival. He had come up the hill on the other side and settled in beside me. He put a large paper bag down next to my left leg. I could hear a mumble and low grinding sounds coming from his teeth.

"What the fuck is he doing?" He was whispering as though he was angry to have to witness this display. Regardless of his outward action, I could tell he was visibly entertained.

"It's Moony." I shrugged without looking at him. I even managed a fake yawn.

"Are you mad, too? Yes, I know it's him. What on earth is he doing? He's trying to catch something. I can't see anything." He stopped and then rolled his eyes, noticing the cloak Moony was wearing. "And he's wearing the heavy priest thing, too. He must be drowning in smelly sweat!"

"I have no idea, Marius. I guess we should see what he's

up to," I said, finally breaking into a chuckle.

"Okay. I'll take the beer with us. You can't trust anyone around here." He was already steps ahead of me and almost running down the hill. If I didn't know any better, I would've guessed he wanted to join Moony's improvisational demonstration or—whatever it was that Moony was doing.

We sauntered down the hill, the aluminum beer cans clanging like cheap church bells in Marius's plastic bag. The tingling sound didn't stop Moony as he continued his motion of leaping high up in the air as if to touch the sky. Finally, we had arrived within mere feet of him when he acknowledged our presence. He barely looked over.

"Guys, I am so happy to see you. Are you here to help me?"

"Help you?" My expression couldn't have been more glazed than if it were a maple donut.

Marius was irritated by my tiptoeing around our curiousness. "He means, what do you think you're doing out here jumping around like an idiot?"

Moony was panting heavily by now. He bent down, almost doubling over his now bent knees. "I heard the news. They said nuclear warheads could arrive here in minutes."

"Nuclear warheads. From where?" I looked at Moony as I bent down to his level. His eyes were wide and almost tearing.

"I was watching the news, and they said the Soviets and U.S. have nuclear missiles that could arrive here in minutes."

"Yes. It's called the Cold War." From my earliest memories, the news my parents watched on TV talked about the race for nuclear supremacy and how if war came, it would mean the end of everything. The sword of Damocles of my generation was this threat. Only this sword was unseen, this fear of something we could not touch or see. Everyone at Pauley High grew up knowing that it could all end suddenly, not with any whimper, instead a true bang. We would likely never even know it was coming until it was too late. Moony appeared to just discover this terrifying new world with its dark secret.

I looked at Moony as Marius walked off, shaking his head in disbelief. He sat himself down and opened a beer as he looked back at me, wanting no part of the discussion. He stayed within earshot, so he truly was interested in his way.

I knelt down in front of Moony and looked at him. "You know, Moony, those missiles can arrive here in minutes. It's true. It just won't happen."

"Really, it won't happen? How can you be sure?"

"Moony, I promise you. I won't let it happen."

"Wow. You certainly seem sure."

"Look, Moony, if I weren't sure, I wouldn't be here at school learning. Who would be learning if there was no future? That would make no sense."

Moony smiled at my logic, satisfying himself with my explanation. "I don't watch much television. I only read books. My aunt had it on and didn't know I was there."

"Don't worry about it, Moony. We've been facing this fear for years." I laughed and walked over to Marius and ruffled his hair. "Does Marius look worried?"

"Marius never looks worried," Moony declared as he stood straight and upright.

"See." I winked at Marius as he pulled back his head to

gulp from the can. Finally, Marius let out a mighty burp and looked at Moony.

"Kiran's right. Listen to him. He's always right." He nodded over to me, the side of his mouth tipped up in a smile. He turned back to Moony. "So, what were you trying to do jumping around like that?"

"I wanted to see how high I could jump and thought maybe if I jumped high enough, well, maybe, I could one day push the moon out of the way in case those missiles were in the sky. I know it makes no sense. It wouldn't hurt trying. Someone has to try to save the moon."

"Makes perfect sense. Now I completely understand." Marius smiled wide, probably entertained by the child in Moony bubbling to the surface. He reached into his bag for another beer and tossed one to me.

"I can't drink. Thanks for offering." Moony protested even before he was offered anything.

"Moony, I would never corrupt you," Marius declared. "I would lose my sanity trying. He, on the other hand, is a different story," he said, gesturing to me.

I took the beer in my hand and sat next to Marius. I gently opened the can and slowly moved my lips toward it. "For God's sake, Wells, it's not like your first kiss. Or is it?" The astuteness of Marius's question injured me.

I ignored the truth behind his question. I wouldn't know the difference since I hadn't had my first kiss yet. Reminded how pathetic that sounded, I quickly took a long sip as my eyes closed at the bitter taste. When I opened them, Moony was smiling at me with his head tilted at an angle.

"If it makes your face go like that, why are you drinking more?"

Marius pulled Moony down next to him and whispered in his ear. "I hope you never find out. I mean that, Moony." He was by now on his second beer and extended his arm around Moony, giving him a squeeze before realizing his indiscretion and withdrawing his arm.

I finished off my first beer and could feel the gas carving its way around my insides, taking up every inch of available space. I knew I would be in trouble if I went for a second beer. The taste in my mouth was foul, and I could imagine my parents smelling it on my breath. I knew I needed to go home soon or else. I thought back up to the top of the hill and how beautiful the view was. Sharing it would be nice. I wondered about it and how nice my first kiss would be up on Shep's Hill.

Finally, I looked up and said, "I probably should head home."

Marius looked across at me with his grin. "You think too much, you know. Fuck it. So it gets dark. Big deal. Won't stop me. I do not get why we cannot do at night what we want to do during the day. Hell. I sleep in most days now that the summer is here."

Moony shifted slowly in his spot, raised his hand to his face, and rubbed his nose slightly. "I never really know what time it is. I mean if the sun didn't go down, I would probably never know when to sleep. Whatever you may think, that's how I see it. I kind of like the dark. Have my best dreams during the night."

Marius stared intently at Moony. "While you are dreaming,

some of us are having a grand old time. You know that, don't you, and I'm sure you're not always dreaming." He reached over to empty the last drops of the third can he was on as if to make a point.

Moony reclined back, his head hitting the grass with a light thud. "The dreams I have get me through the next time I dream again." He closed his eyes as if in a deep sleep and then suddenly sprang up. His head shifted around with a puzzled look in his eyes. I could almost see his eyes rolling from side to side. He shook his head quickly as if moving an idea from one side of his brain to the other.

He suddenly glowered at Marius. "Who's to say that I'm not dreaming, right now? Huh? Wouldn't that be something? I guess you would be messed up, right?" Before Marius could react, he lay back onto the grass and closed his eyes with a look of delirious delight on his face. His smile was wider than a canyon.

Marius sat up and looked at him and me and shook his head, laughing. "Damn right, Moony. I am a figment of your imagination. How messed up is your world then if that is the best you can do?"

Marius and I started laughing and looked up to the sky. A cool breeze swept in from the river, crossing the hill. We all felt it together. Marius looked up at me and said half-jokingly, "What if he is fricken right, and I'm trapped by his imagination?"

I didn't say a word. By then Moony was sound asleep with not a fear in the world.

CHAPTER 15

There is one clear star-filled night I will always remember. We sat at the highest point of Shep's Hill. Although it was not a nightly ritual to bring alcohol up to the shed during the summer, tonight was different. It was the last Friday before summer was officially over for us teens. School would start again on Monday. For some, it would be their final academic year as jobs and the allure of making money would draw them away from academic pursuits. For others, like Marius and myself, it would just be a starting point for a new world: college. No matter, it was our last year as big fish in a small pond. We were arrogant and young as we strode up the hill that night. We actually believed we had mastered the high school world and were ready to ride the waves of our last year in high school.

"Where's Moony?" Marius pondered. "The sun's going down. I don't want to waste our time looking for him in the dark."

"Typical Moony. No watch. No time. Just whatever beat he was synched with. Are the others coming?"

"Argh!" He swept his arm out dismissively as if slapping away three-hundred-pound flies. "After last time, I don't expect them to show. I mean, especially since I told them we would have libations."

The last time was a month ago. Dale had brought beer, or so he called it, that he and the crew had been "manufacturing" in their parents' basement. Dale's dad supposedly helped. The beer tasted like, as Marius politely described it, "foul-tasting urine." Enough of us got sick that many were in parental lockdown for a time after and presumably still were. No one dared ask Marius what "good-tasting urine" tasted like, as just the thought of it would conjure up bad memories. I noticed no difference between the first and the last time I had a beer.

"Did you bring some drink?" Marius asked with a worried look.

"Yes, yes. I got this from my dad's stash. He'll never know it's missing. Someone gave it to him a couple of years ago. I remember how excited he pretended to be and then he hid it, saying he would never touch the stuff."

"Absinthe." Marius stared at the ovular-shaped green bottle. "Will this stuff kill us?"

"I doubt it, but I think you can trip out if you have too much."

Marius held the bottle in his hands and tossed it gently from one hand to another. He seemed bemused yet perplexed.

"One shot each, right?"

Marius continued to inspect the bottle. Flipping it up and down and even mildly shaking it.

"Right?" I repeated.

"Yeah, sure," he gingerly stated as though catching himself.

We could hear footsteps crunching behind us on the moist grass. We didn't have to look behind us to know who it was.

We could even hear the slithering of heavy material along the ground.

"Good lord! He's wearing the cape again. All summer, he ditched that bloody thing, and he has to bring it tonight."

The footsteps grew closer and closer while the slither got louder and clumsier.

"Play along, Marius, please. He sincerely believes he's a shaman, you know, and who is to say he's not…" I winked. Moony had come a long way, or so I thought. I never ventured to guess it was the other way around.

"Sorry I'm late," Moony said. "I waited for the sun to go down. I didn't want to be up here with it glaring in my eyes. I would be pretty blinded."

Marius broke out in laughter. "Ah, Moony, the sun will never defeat you. You have magical powers. Only you do not know what they are yet." He laughed himself into a seating position on the hill and looked up at the stars. We looked at each other and joined him with our legs folded across and for the next few minutes, we enjoyed the silence.

Marius broke the silence finally. "All right, get out the hooch. I'm going to be an old man before we drink."

Moony piped up. "If it's alcohol, I can't drink it. If you poison my mind, I won't be able to lead."

Marius winked at me. "No problem, Moony. I think it's just green apple cider from Europe. It is heavy shit, but that's because the apples were bitter when squeezed."

I whipped out three small Styrofoam cups and gave Marius a hefty frown over the lie he just told.

With a small gesture of his fingers made it clear that a

little wouldn't hurt.

I poured as little as I could into Moony's cup. If he spontaneously combusted, at least the trace would be small. I poured much more for Marius and myself. As I handed Marius's cup to him, he looked at me defiantly.

"When did you become my mom?" he bellowed, reaching for the bottle.

I pulled the bottle back and preempted his coming tirade.

"A toast, boys! To us and our upcoming last year of high school. We pledge to work hard sometimes, and play hard all the time. To all our friends, Romans, and countrymen who could not be here, to all those about to graduate . . . Cheers!"

I stood up at full military attention and saluted the town and our school below.

Moony and Marius followed, standing up. Marius hailed but Moony had the distant look he sometimes got. Instead of saluting, he looked over at me and smiled and, with a cup in hand, greeted the stars.

Within seconds, the reaction to the drink hit us like an earthquake shaking a feather hut.

"Holy shit, you trying to kill us? Wow. This stuff is wicked." Marius staggered back and forth lurching his chest and shoulders forward. He turned his feet sideways and wobbled deliberately. He was enjoying his act. "I definitely need more."

The taste was intoxicating. I could feel the fumes chisel their way straight to my head. As Marius reached for the bottle, I quickly threw it at a protruding rock a few feet away. The bottle shattered like a cymbal hit by twelve drummers at once.

Marius looked at me with his eyes lowered, his lips tight together, and shaking his head.

"Marius, if we drank the whole thing, we wouldn't be going back down this hill. Sorry. I didn't realize how potent it was."

We hadn't noticed Moony during this. He slowly backed away and sat under a tree, his eyes glazed and now fixed upon the sky. It probably was the first time his lips had touched alcohol. I was scared as I watched him.

"You alive?"

"I'm fine, but I hear voices. I think the stars are talking to me," he said, obviously not wanting to converse as he averted making eye contact. Totally preoccupied in his trance.

"What are you seeing, I mean, hearing? Do you need help?"

"No. Everything is clear. The stars are dancing in front of me. It's quite beautiful the way they're calling my name, like in a chant. Quite relaxing and peaceful."

Moony slowly started shuffling his feet and dancing to his tune. Moony demonstrated a rhythm I would never have believed he had. I could see Marius's look of horror as I joined in with Moony doing a punk type of dance. Our arms and feet stomped. Our bodies gyrated violently led by our heads bobbing from side to side. All this without any music.

"Freaksters. Damn freaksters," Marius declared. He put down his cup and began his own dance. Grooving his hips back and front. The moonlight was blinding as it shone on us.

I could almost feel a soft vibration of the light as it settled on my face during my dance.

Moony started swaying side to side and had made himself dizzy. Marius began to laugh as he swung his cross over his neck and ignored Moony's condition.

"Do you hear the same thing?" Moony said. "The voice calling to me. It's my voice coming from the stars and speaking to me."

"Really?" Marius said, puzzled as I took a step back to observe.

"What's the voice saying, Moony? What's the voice saying to you?" My voice cracked—I was both anxious and fearful of his response.

"That I'm on the right path and should continue to follow the path I shall choose. It is my voice. My voice!" Moony kept repeating that mantra until he slowly drifted off to sleep on his own feet. Marius and I supported him so he wouldn't fall.

"I guess we need to take him home."

"What, ring the doorbell and run? Fuck. Imagine what his aunt will do if he's like this. She might kill us for damaging him!"

"Let's wait it out until he wakes up. I gave him barely a teaspoon."

Marius started laughing. "Our last night of freedom and here we are with a guy who hears voices, gets—wasted on a tiny sip from some strange drink, while wearing a dress! Man, that is enough crap to get me through this year."

I looked at Moony as Marius snorted loudly, as if a memory popped into his head like a red flag in front of an angry bull.

"Remember how in religion class, we were talking about the second coming and how would we ever know the Messiah arrived?"

"Yeah and I remember Moony raising his hand to give Father Satler his two cents."

"Moony said we should spend less time waiting for the second coming and more time searching for him here."

"Right . . . on earth."

"Moony never said on earth. He said here in class."

"Who cares? Here, there, everywhere, today, tomorrow. Moony always says things to stir things up. Like all this voice stuff. Of course, he heard a voice. How could it not be his own? He is non-stop talking and cannot hear anyone else!"

Eventually, Moony awoke, not remembering a thing and went on his way back home.

"What a wonderful night this was. I cannot wait to start the school year," he said as he strolled down the hill.

Marius walked over to me. "Thanks for not telling him he heard voices. We would have never gotten him home."

"It's getting late. We should call it a night."

Marius raised his empty cup. "To us and the havoc we will wreak!"

I picked up my cup and raised it slowly. "To the future." I lowered my cup and it slipped out of my hand as a severe gust of wind blew across the hill.

I walked down the hill with Marius, desperately wanting to tell him, but each time held back, second-guessing what I heard or not.

Moony was not the only one who heard a voice. The voice I heard spoke to me and it was not a voice I recognized. The voice was ageless and echoed through the hollowness of my mind. Before I went to sleep, I wrote what I heard so

I wouldn't forget it and put the paper in my pillowcase. A perfect place and complementary to what had been going on within my subconscious for a time preceding it.

The voice told me that true love would burn me from the inside out. If I dare not open my lips to let the smoke from this fire escape, I would suffocate.

CHAPTER 16

That same night, I dreamt of a voice that calmed my soul and I kept dreaming of it until school started in September. The face and body behind the voice were never clear. What exactly happened in the dream was a pleasant mystery. There was the sound and the feeling of complete contentment of my soul that followed. There was no time nor space. I could sense the presence of two of us holding hands, one being mine and one feminine, although I couldn't see her. There was no doubt that it was a girl.

Who was I dreaming of? There was someone there. It was a voice I hadn't heard and one that reached out only to me. Moony would take it to the nth degree, setting him off on a twenty-day monologue. I couldn't let that happen. Marius would certainly laugh and only stop to take a break to laugh some more. He would tell me it was just a stupid dream.

It would have been easy to dismiss it in some ways, and much more comfortable if I did dismiss it. However, there was more to it—much more. How many more times I dreamt a similar dream over the next few nights, I lost track. Some mornings I would wake up trying to recall and could not. Then a moment would come and go. A sequence would play within my mind that could only come from a dream. The voice was always the same. It was feminine and young.

My age, or pretty close. I couldn't make out any physical form to go with it. When it played back in the mind, there was something about it that was special—that I could not describe at that time. I did know when I dreamt I felt more awake than when the alarm sounded. It was pure contentment with the world.

I wondered if it was the alcohol from the late night at the park, but sometimes the dreams would come when I hadn't been drinking with the boys. I didn't know what to do, but I went to bed those nights with great anticipation. There was always the fear, though, that the dreams would stop one day.

By the time the new school year started, I had gently tucked away this little fantasy of mine into a box with a pretty bow in the back closet of my mind. The last Friday night up on the hill, I was tempted to unwrap the box. I chose not to.

The first day of my senior year, I woke up and got ready like I always did. But that day was different than all the rest, in more ways than one. I had been relieved of music duties, which alleviated the burden of carrying anything more than my notebook. I took a glance at the large radio with its well-worn cassette buttons sitting on a chair in the far corner of my room. It had served my rise to credibility well.

While I got dressed in blue jeans and a boring shirt, I wondered what everyone else would be wearing. Janie and her group would be pure punk. A guessing game ensued revolving around whether her hair would be colored or not, and, if so, what shade.

It was also the day my parents left the blue NASA jacket for me to find. After putting it on, I ran through the park with reckless abandon.

Summer was enjoying its last glory, and there was a hint of an autumn wind. Thomas had already left, as I was late. The ground was moist from a late-night shower. I was in full gallop as I saw the pack assembled near the sandbox by the kiddie section of the park.

"Kiran, what the heck, man? What took you so long?" said Dale, wearing a vintage Zappa T-shirt. "No radio?"

"Not my turn this year."

Thomas quickly interjected. "This one is on Marius. Where is he?"

I could hear the footsteps coming up behind. I recognized the shrill wail that was Janie's voice.

"Cool jacket. Almost punk. Not quite. Almost."

"Thanks." Her hair color was a dark brown now, with some green and blue streaks. It was slightly longer than last year, yet still no river of wheat from her youth. "Don't want to get in trouble first day, right," I said laughingly.

"Yep. Tomorrow, it's all blue."

"I know you don't smoke so I won't bother you." She was on a mission. She and her posse moved on ahead, as usual, trying to shakedown anyone who smoked. "Remind me to get that album *Evol* from you. You have it?" I knew, like the changing of the seasons, she would eventually ask to borrow something.

"Yeah. I do. I'll bring it tomorrow."

"Well, the bell rings in like ten minutes. We can't wait for Marius all day."

"Maybe he was expelled."

"Naw, he would still show. Shit. He would be early, I'm guessing."

Suddenly, we could hear it. Long before we could see Marius and his ghetto blaster coming down the hill from the other side of the park, the trademark sound of The Who punched holes in the air as he approached.

Before we could sing the next line, Marius came thundering down the hill, backpack, construction boots, and all, singing the climatic verse from "Bargain", before contorting his body into a semi-drum roll and guitar windmill.

"Wow. Wellsie. You finally decided to dress up for school. That is a great-looking jacket. What the hell are you guys doing? We'll be late." He pumped up the volume even higher and led the charge.

I trailed behind, waiting for Moony to catch up. He lived off of the far side of the park. Coming from the opposite end, he would pass through the woods to meet us here. I wondered if they cut off the passageway through the woods. They had some little kids getting lost in there this past summer.

I finally saw Moony appear out of the forest. He made it a point to tell me that what he was wearing was the same cloak. We noticed how sparingly he wore it under the summer's sun. It was smaller on him now, as even he had grown. No longer did it reach down to touch the ground as he walked. The brown leather straps that hung down from the satchel he wore to carry his books were worn and weather-beaten, giving it a certain charm.

"Looks good, Moony," I said, waving my hand at his cloak. "You've grown into it. Looks much better on you. Hopefully, you won't trip on it all year."

He laughed as he usually did, hysterically with his head careening up and down.

We made our way into the school when the opening bell sounded, a feeling of total exhilaration swept across me. This was it. My last year in high school, and I felt like I owned the universe. I gave a small fist pump to myself and then entered what I thought was my kingdom for one last glorious year.

I made my way to the locker bay and passed by Marius's locker in the row just behind mine. We shared the same classes and in between took stock of how the day was progressing, laughing at the teachers and classmates we had and how easy this year would be.

Marius pointed his finger at me. "Do well, buddy. You have to get into the same college as me."

It was all a total ruse and Marius's way of reminding me of my mission. I knew I would have to work hard to help Marius get through, and the average he needed would not be a sure thing. I was confident, though, since I helped him get by last winter, and he was in most of my classes this year. Moony got nineties, or so we imagined. He told us he was going to college wherever we were. Over the summer, we never spoke about any other school other than the nearby college. In our circle, no one thought they had the financial means to entertain any other options.

"Well, one more class to go, English literature," I declared.

"Cool. Do I have time to smoke?"

"No, you can wait 'til after school. Let's not be late for anything the first day."

"I was going to tell you about the girls. There's talk, you know. A couple girls think you look good in your new jacket."

"Really," I said, half mocking as I mimicked Marius's inflection. "They just like the jacket."

"Hell no. C'mon dude. It's the man in the jacket." He poked me on the shoulder and started shaking his head. "I do *not* know what it is with you and girls. Seriously. You are so difficult when it comes to chicks. There are girls out there who like you, you know."

"Aw man. Let me just enjoy my year." I could tell he was annoyed because he rolled his eyes clockwise and counter-clockwise for emphasis. He knew that despite my bravado with the guys, I was scared shitless.

"Why are you taking your jacket to English class?"

"I figured since it was last period we can take off right after school without coming back to our lockers."

He quickly reached into his locker to pull out his red-and-black-squared lumberjack coat and put it under his arms. "Good idea. Now don't you even want to know about Janie's friend who . . . ?"

"Leave it alone, Marius. Leave it alone."

"Damn. They have to bite him on the fricken rear end to wake him up." He pretended to mumble.

"I heard that."

"Sorry."

I laughed and stopped abruptly. The pretty bow on the box deep in the closet seemed to undo slowly. I strained my thoughts through a silk filter hoping to recall the melody of that voice about to escape. Panic swept over me. I could not recall that voice anymore. I just knew that there was a dream. The voice was gone.

I trembled ever so slightly as one would at the onset of a fever. *It was gone.* It was like some cruel joke. I could no longer recall the dream or that voice of calm or comfort. Why I suddenly wanted to hear that voice, those soft flowing waves, I didn't know. Maybe it was the thought of a girl being interested in me. I longed for the voice, that one voice to be conjured up. Like the eighteenth-century pirates burying their treasures on a distant shore only to return to find the box empty, I felt the pulp sucked out from my gut.

I noticed Marius looking back, obviously wondering why I slowed down, so I stepped up my pace. In doing so, my mind moved back to the here and now. I had hidden away the box for too long, and now everything in it vanished. I was briefly yet quite profoundly sad for a reason I didn't understand.

Before I knew it, we had reached our English lit class, with Marius scampering on ahead so he could get the last seat at the back of the class. I could see him throw his backpack on the desk directly in front. I knew immediately what that meant. It was my preordained seat.

Suddenly leaping out in front of me was Moony.

"Something wrong, bad day?"

"No. No. Um . . . I just left something at home, is all. Forgot where I put it. You know how it is."

He smiled back. "Today is a good day. The first day."

"Of course, the first day of school. Great day so far."

Moony grinned and retreated to the first available seat

at the front of the class. I bumped into the first desk and dropped my backpack and jacket. I knelt down to pick up the pens and pencils that spewed out and reassembled the books I dropped.

While I was kneeling down, I could hear the banter of the students proceeding in. Some were introducing themselves to the teacher. Then, as if the earth had suddenly stopped spinning, a gentle, soft feminine voice rose and found its way through the din of the shrill and deep voices occupying the classroom space to my welcoming ear.

"Mrs. Woodsmith. I noticed we'll be doing poetry. Will we be studying the works of T. S. Eliot?"

"Yes. Indeed."

"'The Love Song of J. Alfred Prufrock'?" The voice was hesitant, each word becoming more of a whisper than the previous.

"Yes, why do ask? You seem concerned."

"Well, I was wondering, if you know, I mean, if all the works we would be studying would be, you know . . . bleak," she said plaintively.

I could hear Mrs. Woodsmith get up from the desk and move closer to her.

"Ah. It's all how you interpret them," she said laughingly. "For sure, we will study others that are very romantic and much more upbeat."

"I do enjoy Eliot, too." I could hear the footsteps move away to the far corner of the room.

The voice was unmistakable. It was the voice, tone for tone, vibration for vibration, the voice of my dreams. It was beyond a doubt. With each word she uttered, I studied every syllable in my mind and replayed it a million times in the seconds she spoke.

My hands were trembling uncontrollably, and a shiver went from my toes to my spine. I was scared to lift my head. It was a voice I recognized and didn't recognize at the same time. It hadn't lived in my world until now, only in my dreams. The voice now drifted in waves across the very air I breathed. The deeply buried box had opened and the gift given for my private world to enjoy. No wonder it had been emptied minutes earlier.

My eyes betrayed me; I looked. I mean, I had to. Across the room, I could see the long, flowing black hair all the way below her shoulders and midway down her back. She arrived at the last available seat at the opposite end of the classroom. It was at the rear of the class directly opposite Marius. When she turned to sit, she looked up at the board. She had the prettiest dark eyes I had ever seen. Her face was small and angular and perfectly formed. I stared at her lips, hoping they would open so I could hear the voice again. She wore small black-framed glasses that reflected like a diamond as the sunlight hit them.

Suddenly, Mrs. Woodsmith addressed me. "Have your seat, Mr. Wells," she cooed. "I believe your friend has saved you one."

"Right," I said, wondering if the whole world had seen my staring and if my secret had been betrayed. I realized what for me was forever had happened quickly. While I made my way to my seat, I carefully avoided gazing at the other side of the class. I took one last look as I spun in my seat. She was certainly real. She was definitely there, and she was the most beautiful girl I had ever seen.

I took a bottomless and steady breath.

I had never felt this way before. My heart raced as if trying to leave my body. My thoughts danced around the image I could now frame in my mind. I could think of nothing else at that moment and all moments going forward. The whole world seemed suddenly different and new, as if a treasure had suddenly been revealed only to me.

I felt alive. At the same time, in the depths of my heart now, I felt the distance in the physical world between us. I was still on one side of the classroom, and this stunning girl who rose to life from my dreams was only twenty feet or so away from me. It might as well have been light years. The frustrating search for the theory of everything within a teen-age soul is how the scientist would document my frustration.

I had to trade places. I had to be able to look at her. I couldn't right now. I had to have Marius's seat, though I could never tell him exactly why. He would ruin it for me or think I was infantile. Very quietly and calmly, I whispered to Marius, "Want to change seats? I can see fine from the back."

"You must be joking. I like to sit here. I can see your answers from here." He put his big construction boots up on the radiator at the back of the class. "See, I need a good warm footrest." I was about to push the subject and stopped short. He would find it strange. Besides, Mrs. Woodsmith was starting to go through the attendance and I had to find out who the girl was.

Name after name went and nothing.

Kiran Wells.

"Present."

Laura Winters.

"Present."

There was the voice. Laura Winters. The name rolled on top of the voice in my mind. I searched the depths of my memory and could not come up with the name. She had never been in any of my classes in high school until now. *Was she new?* That would explain a lot.

The bell rang. The class, seemingly, had only lasted mere seconds. I planned to wait and let Laura leave first so I could watch discreetly at the safest of distances. Unfortunately, Marius was poking at me.

"Hurry up, slowpoke. Let's get out of here. Remember, you wanted to get out fast."

"Yup, correct," I said, and before I knew it, I was shoved out the door and out of the school.

Desperately, I tried to look back to find her in the parade of people leaving the school. We went to the park and shot the shit for hours. Or, at least, the guys did. Conversations bounced around me and off of me, but I was in my own world.

After everyone else went home, I lingered for a while by myself. I slowly made my way up to the top of the hill that overlooked the river nearby. I could hear the water running and wave after wave flowing by me. On the horizon, the sun shone bright orange and in the backdrop, I could see the moon emerging slowly from the clouds. I thought of the girl with the voice, the eyes, the hair, and the name, Laura Winters, and somehow while on that hill, it all seemed so simple and peaceful.

I thanked my mom and dad for the jacket again that night and ran to my room. The next day could not come fast enough. I prepared my bed and fluffed my pillows, hoping to welcome any dream seeking shelter in my subconscious.

CHAPTER 17

Invigorated from a blissful sleep, for the first time in my life, I looked forward to being at school as opposed to enjoying the journey there. I pleaded to the heavens the preceding night that this was not some cruel nightmare and that Laura Winters existed.

Marius walked with me to school that morning, cautiously interrogating me. "You're acting differently. Why are you in such a rush?"

I knew I had to scale it back. I couldn't tell Marius much. He wouldn't understand. He'd been on my case since I met him. *How could I explain that I read poetry at home and enjoyed T. S. Eliot? How could I explain that I could never tell anyone that or why I felt scared?* Then suddenly comes this girl who gets poetry, has been in my dreams, and is now in my class. This year of all years. I was dying to ask about her. I needed to know everything about her, and if anyone knew her. I couldn't afford to have anyone becoming suspicious of me.

"It's the weather. It is such a gorgeous day out, and I had a good night's sleep. That's all. Look, there's Moony. I need to ask him something." I ran over to Moony near the entrance of the school. Even if he got suspicious, he wouldn't say anything. He had his litany of things to talk

about first. No one would be able to decipher the riddle
when he spoke, thankfully.

"Hey, Moony, did you notice how many new kids there are
in school this year? A few transferred in, eh?" I rattled off a
list of two to three newcomers before I strategically added,
"And some girl named Laura, maybe Winters?"

"Hmm. Yeah, there are some new ones this year. Hey,
remember when I was the new kid? Wow. Seems like yesterday." You could see his mind drift off into another orbit.
I reached out to his thought bubble, trying to pull it back
toward me.

"Yeah. Do you know anything about them?"

He went through the names I mentioned and went on
and on about what he knew.

"And what about Laura Winters? You didn't mention her."

"No, she's not new. She was in a couple of my classes last
year. I think she always went to this school."

I was dumbfounded while my heart slightly sank. *She
had been in this school all this time!* "I've never seen her, so
I thought she was new. I wonder where she lives, because I
haven't seen her around."

"She's a busser. Lives over on the other side of town."

"You know her?" Now I knew I was tempting fate with
these questions.

"Not really. She keeps to herself. I know she likes to read
and stuff. She was in one of my group projects. Maybe
I should talk to her more," he said, seemingly making a
mental note.

I laughed expressively, wearing a smile almost bigger than

my face could bear, hoping to throw him off the trail. "You already talk to too many people."

Well, she was real and so close to me all these years. My mind raced. *Was she a nice girl? What did she enjoy reading?* Millions of things I wanted to know.

English class was the first period today. The sun was bright and lit up the room as I entered. There she was in her seat, head down and writing. She looked up to copy something that was on the board. Her eyes were a deep dark black, and I was losing myself in them. I found myself smiling, and it took every fiber of my being to take my eyes off her and sit down. Marius soon came by and bounced his notepad off my head.

Class started and we were given various works of poetry to read and analyze before discussing them. I was zoning out until I heard Mrs. Woodsmith say Laura's name. "Yes, Laura."

"I think the writer is trying to say that there are things more powerful and meaningful than our material world."

"Good point. Anyone else?"

Laura's voice lifted me out of my chair. I read the poem and thought about what she said. I was not worthy of this. All I could see on the page were words.

"Marius. What do you think the poet's message is?" Once again, Marius was obviously uninterested, maybe daydreaming, and had been caught. Daydreaming was not the appropriate word. Marius was likely listening to some soundtrack running through his mind.

"Know what? I see a lot of words and the poet is trying to make a living, so he was trying to explain why the world is evil. He really should just say that."

Mrs. Woodsmith smirked and then, horrors of all horrors, looked directly at me.

"Do you agree, Mr. Wells?"

I was startled. "Agree with who?"

"Your friend." She motioned with her hand in the direction behind me, and I quickly looked back at Marius and knew I was in bottomless trouble. Now Marius was smiling profusely. He was fully expecting me to play straight man to his court jester. However, to this day, I do not know how I found the words, but they came to me.

"Well, I tend to think the poet has these strong feelings and emotions about the material world. Emotions and feelings shouldn't be broken down to one or two words. I'm not sure if words even exist that can capture the soul's desires." I stopped and tried to wait for my brain to put an end to this runaway train.

"Go on, Mr. Wells."

"Yes. Go on, Mr. Wells," Marius chirped from behind, clearly realizing the punchline was not coming.

"The feelings and emotions a poet wants to convey are those that we feel when we read the words. He has to put them in a way to get us to find the emotions buried within us. So because we're all different, we get different emotions from what we read…" I paused for a freaking long time and added, "I think."

"Does that help, Marius?"

I turned to look at Marius. I felt both sheepish and surprised by what had come out from me. He had a smirk on his face. "Yes. Clear as a bell, but I guess the world sucks would be too simple to write."

While everyone looked at Marius as he talked, my eyes drifted across the room. Laura was smiling. I had seen her smile, and she smiled at what I had said. There was a brief moment where our eyes may have met. However, I moved my gaze away so fast, I'll never know for sure. Seeing that smile set my heart ablaze with joy. She smiled at my words— my point of view. I was so ecstatic, and I felt complete. There was little doubt now.

I took out an empty notebook and wrote.

Yesterday I fell in love. Today my world went from stick people and black and white to form and color.

When the bell rang to end the period, the students got up to leave. Mrs. Woodsmith called out over the din. "Mr. Wells, if you have a second, I would like to speak to you."

Marius laughed. "Smartass. Now you'll have to teach the class."

I waited for everyone to leave. My head was down, and I was suddenly embarrassed.

"Mr. Wells. You were in my class a couple of years back, right?"

"Yes. Ma'am."

"Well, you've obviously read more literature than you have let on."

"I guess so."

"Don't be shy to express your ideas and speak out."

I stood there and nodded my head. There was a long pause, and Mrs. Woodsmith started to pack her things.

"Sometimes, the words don't come to me. I mean, to say things at the right time."

"Well, you did quite well today."

"I guess I had a good day today."

She looked intently at me. "Try this. Write your thoughts down as they come. A little trick I learned. It may help."

"Like a diary," I said dismissively.

"No. It doesn't have to be formal. Write when you want to write. It can be about anything at all. I think it might help you find that voice within you."

"Well . . . thanks," I said. "I have to get going to chemistry. Thanks. I appreciate it."

She smiled at me. "By the way, don't expect everyone to understand you, either."

"Right."

I did appreciate it. From then on, I always had pen and notebook close by. It was also the only way I knew how to share the pure feelings of love I felt. I had awakened to a strange new and elegant world that welcomed my presence.

The writing became an obsession. Wherever I went, the notepad would be close by and carefully guarded, especially around Marius. I used the excuse that I was taking notes for a particular class or that I was becoming forgetful and needed to write things down. One thing I never did was go back and reread whatever I wrote. Lines of paper were filled and not returned to—like unrequited love, I suppose.

Marius was the first to notice that I had become more introverted, or even more so than I usually was. I sat and listened, but partook in carrying the discussions less and less. When we met after school, I heard the usual complaints about parents, teachers, what so and so was wearing, and all of the day-to-day trials and tribulations of a teenager. We would often tease each other, and even at that, I withdrew. I should say I was content through all this. I would enjoy the streams of communications flowing through me. I just couldn't throw myself into their ways as I had been swept about into another universe.

The air was starting to grow colder, and leaves would soon be completely off the trees. The after-school rituals of late summer would ultimately be put on hold only to return during the springtime, once the snow had melted.

I would see Laura in and around the school at a distance. I would gaze and try not to stare as she boarded the bus home. I looked forward to every English class and devoting my ears to her voice when she spoke. I mastered the technique of adjusting my chair and turning to talk to Marius while glancing over at her. As weird as it seemed, knowing she and I shared this universe was enough for now.

Moony had noticed all my scribbling and the notebook I was carrying. He told me he received a new backpack for his birthday and offered me his weather-beaten auburn-colored satchel. I accepted the offer and now had my own Ark of the Covenant to carry the words that meant so much to me.

CHAPTER 18

It was a crisp autumn evening. A perfect setting for Halloween night. Snow had not fallen yet, and it was unseasonably warm. A large contingent of us had met at the base of the hill with loot bags and makeshift costumes. Moony's transition was smooth. He found a pointed cap, a plastic wand, and went as a wizard. Was he Merlin or Gandalf or who knows what? Nobody dared to ask. The accompanying literature lesson from Moony would likely go on, until Christmas if we did. We were too old for ordinary trick-or-treating, so we went out later in the evening under the cover of darkness after the young ones had long since retired. Bags of chips were our favorite treat.

Marius showed up in cowboy boots, a jean jacket, and a black cowboy hat with a kerchief around his neck. He had a metal toy gun in one hand.

"You Jesse James?" asked Thomas, who, like he did every Halloween that I could recollect, dressed as a football player.

Marius gave him an eye roll before introducing his persona. "I'm going as a sheriff, a U.S. marshal."

"Why the black hat? Good guys don't wear black hats." It was Dale interjecting from beneath his makeshift ghost/bedsheet costume.

"They wear black now, and who says I have to be a good

guy, right, Moony?"

Moony looked up at Marius lamentingly with his eyes open wide. "If you say so."

I knew the attention would turn to me at some point.

"Who the fuck are you supposed to be, Mercutio?" We had been reading *Romeo and Juliet* that week, so Marius's comments were much more intelligent than they may have appeared.

I was wearing a flowing white shirt (one of my dad's oversized dress shirts), slightly puffy at the sleeves, and pajama bottoms. Over the top of my shirt was an old white tablecloth with a hole cut out to fit my head through. Across the middle of the tablecloth was a medieval cross that I had carefully drawn in bright red.

"Medieval knight," I said, making sure I pointed out my sword to them. It was a blunt old sword that I had back in the day when I went as a pirate.

Moony moved in close for inspection. "A Templar Knight. That's what you are. You know they were all slaughtered by the church? Very brave of you to wear!"

I laughed at Moony. "No need to worry about that. I'm glad you like it."

Marius shook his head. "Pajama bottoms. Seriously? You look like that damn Mercutio guy or maybe even his friend." He grabbed my sword and stepped away from the assembled group that now stood before him. He pointed the sword, not menacingly but tauntingly, at me.

"True, I talk of dreams,

Which are the children of an idle brain,
Begot of nothing but vain fantasy."

He gave me the sword back and smiled. "You thought I don't pay attention. Right, Romeo?"

"Umm . . . no, you just memorized the lines that we all had to," I said, trying to poke holes in this victorious bubble he had created for himself. I laughed as I took the sword back and put it in the makeshift sling I made to carry it.

We broke off into pairs and went into the residential neighborhoods surrounding our school and crisscrossed streets to do so, promising to return to the park to divvy up our loot and trade at the end of the night.

It was around 11 p.m, and the moon hid amongst the threatening clouds. The forecasted rain remained at bay mercifully, so we could properly pillage our small town. The gang had returned after a good hour of trading. Marius hadn't come back to the park yet. He had made us promise not to leave until he got there. We guessed he had probably followed some girls along the way and was playing his U.S. marshal routine to the hilt. One thing about Marius was that he always showed up eventually, especially if there was some new conquest to divulge. He always needed his audience.

Moony yawned repeatedly. His eyes darted chaotically while looking to the sky as if he was trying to see through and in between clouds. He loved watching the sky at night. He claimed if he tried hard enough, he could set his mind to visiting the stars and the moon.

I once asked if he meant just using his imagination. He

firmly believed that he could leave his body and visit faraway places by only thinking about them intensely. I would sit and smile as he did this. My thoughts were not to the heavens but on one person here on earth.

Suddenly, Moony became restless. Something caught his gaze in the distance. He was like a guard dog sensing an unwelcome presence. "Kiran! Someone just went into the cabin up there."

He was referring to the old cabin about forty feet into the woods near the top of the hill. "I saw someone going in there. I think I should check it out. Maybe someone's lost."

"Moony, I hate to break it you but it might just be, you know, people who want to be alone. I mean, it is a great quiet spot and much warmer than you know . . ."

"What? I'm not sure I understand."

I took an elongated pause as if to clear my throat. There was no way I was going to have a father-and-son talk with Moony.

"Just forget about it. I hope Marius gets here soon. I'm freezing."

Moony got up suddenly. "I'm going to see what's going on. Maybe someone's lost. Those woods are gloomy and pretty thick."

"C'mon, Moony. If they went to the cabin, they're quite fine in many ways."

"No. I have a bad feeling about this. Someone might need our help." He started walking at a quick pace to the cabin and I scrambled to get up and follow him.

"Damn. I'll come with you."

I finally caught up with him as we got within a few feet of the cabin. There were voices coming from inside. It was completely black, and I could see a splattering or flash of light from inside. Whoever was inside was using a flashlight.

I tried to pull on Moony's outfit to stop him. I didn't want to yell and attract attention; I had a sick feeling in my stomach. Suddenly, Moony took off in front of me and burst through the door. "Is everybody okay?" Within seconds, a body threw himself at Moony and tackled him through the doorway back toward me. My fake sword went flying to the ground. As I scrambled to turn around and retrieve my senses, two figures stood menacingly over me.

Both had on black leather jackets and jeans. Both wore old work boots. I could see their faces clearly as they towered over me. They weren't much taller than me. Unmistakeable were their shaved heads. I recognized the piercing gray eyes of the taller one. His name was Robbie Dialto. He dropped out of our school more than a year ago. The other guy must have been his friend Drey who got expelled with him. They were caught peddling drugs to the younger grades. Both were skinheads or dressed the role, whatever, it didn't matter.

"Wells! I remember you." Robbie studied me carefully.

"We went to elementary school together." I slowly started getting up.

"You know these geeks?" The other voice spoke.

"Only this one." Robbie pointed his finger at my chest. I could see the other hand reaching into his back pocket. I could see a knife handle sticking out of Robbie's jacket. My heart started racing.

"We thought someone needed help. No one hangs around this cabin and . . ."

"Mind your fuckin' business next time. Or next time will be the last time. Understand?" Drey stepped in front of Robbie and pushed me hard. I'm not sure if he was trying to provoke me or just scare me. I stumbled back and luckily caught my footing. My eyes fixated on their hands and their back pockets. I could see Moony in the background sitting up with his mouth wide open and trembling. He had rolled to the side when he got tackled. For an instant, they forgot him.

"I got it. We didn't mean anything. Sorry. We'll just go."

Drey turned to Robbie and motioned for him to look over at Moony.

"Look at this freak. He dresses like a five year old."

"Leave him alone." The words came instinctively out of me.

Both of them turned to me now and glared ominously with hands reaching into their pockets. I held my ground and could see Moony was distracted. A figure was running at a frantic pace. I recognized the heavy footsteps and could hear the thumping on the moist October grass. I backed up slightly and rambled on, talking as I kept stepping back. They continued to move toward me and were so saturated with rage that they didn't hear the footsteps thundering behind them.

"Run, Moony. Run! Go home. Fast!" I wanted to get him out of harm's way.

Moony grabbed his loot bag and ran in the opposite direction just as Marius appeared in full flight. As they turned to chase Moony, Marius rose full force through the air, swifter than a tiger through a circus hoop, and landed a ferocious elbow into Drey's face. Blood splattered all over Marius's jean jacket as he landed on top of him. I impulsively grabbed Robbie at the knees and tackled him before he could get to Marius. In no time, Marius was up in full vigor and onto Robbie's back, flipping him over and pinning him to ground. His fists never stopped pumping. In the background, Drey covered his blood-drenched face with his hands and retreated quickly into the cabin and came out with a couple of small sandwich bags containing a powdery substance and ran off into the woods. I reached around Marius's arms to stop the assault. He finally stopped and got up off of Robbie.

"Skinhead creep. Get the fuck out of here and never come back," he barked into Robbie's face. Robbie got up and took off in the direction of Drey and off into the woods.

"Where's Moony?" Marius said, looking around.

"He took off the other way. I'm pretty sure he went home," I said while studying Marius.

"Now what are you looking at it?"

"I just never saw you so angry. You were going to kill him, weren't you?"

"No. I would have stopped punching. Eventually."

The display of brutality and anger both intrigued and saddened me. I was at the time grateful that Marius had arrived because I'm not sure what might have happened.

"Shit. Sorry about your jacket," I said. I walked along the route from where Marius had come and picked up the black cowboy hat he had worn.

"Man…." We walked back together through the park.

"Thanks, Marius," I said, punching him on the shoulder as I headed toward my house.

I looked back to see Marius checking his clothes for blood and shaking his head.

***

The next day, I gave Marius the old World War Two fighter jacket I had. It had always been a little bit big on me and, frankly, I never wore it anymore.

"Thanks. I always liked it. You don't have to."

"Nope. It never quite fit, and I owe you big time. Consider it an early Christmas gift."

At lunch the next day, we recounted our adventure to the cafeteria table. Moony sat quietly and detached.

"Hey, Moony," Dale said. "What were you doing while all this was going on?" He started laughing.

Moony smiled and looked at me sheepishly. "Kiran told me to run, so I ran."

The table broke out in laughter.

I leaned across to Moony and whispered to him. "Moony, you did a good thing. Whenever you're in trouble, please run. Promise me."

"Aw. You're a great friend. Run. That's what I'll do if I'm ever in trouble."

CHAPTER 19

Winter came slowly that year, and that was when it happened.

It was last-period English and a light snow had started falling. It was the first snowfall of the year at long last, and a lovely sight. Our classroom had a window looking out on the park. I was talking to Marius before class when out of the corner of my eye, I saw her at the window. *Laura.* I could see her sigh intensely as she admired the snow. She was wearing a white sweater with a Christmas floral decoration across the front. The image was framed indelibly in my mind. Her face against the backdrop of the freshly fallen snow.

Marius caught my gaze. "You are not listening. Pay attention."

"Sorry what . . . I . . . was just . . ."

"What are you staring at?" He turned around slowly, but Laura had fortunately gone to her seat.

"The snow. I was wondering if they had started putting the boards up for the rink."

"Oh," he said.

I felt utterly relieved in that instant. Whether he was buying any of it was a different story.

That class, we were given twenty minutes of reading time. We had been studying *Tender Is the Night* and everyone was to silently read a selected passage.

I usually took advantage of this time to write. I put the novel on the desk to act as a decoy. I also pulled out my notebook to start an impromptu poem, "Laura by the Window." I wrote and wrote, ever forgetful of where I was.

If the snow would dance on your skin,
how would it feel?
If I could touch that snow,
would that not be bold?
My thoughts ripple.
Daydreams spray my peace.
If I could only speak,
I would address such verse to
Laura by the Window.

Suddenly a shadow appeared on my desk and sheer panic spread across my body. It was Mrs. Woodsmith. I sat still and silent, not knowing what to say or do. My eyes were transfixed by the name on the page, "Laura."

Without a word, I quickly slid my notebook under my paperback and started reading. Mrs. Woodsmith said nothing and tapped me gently on the shoulder. I kept my head down with my hands holding on to the book for dear life. She walked back to her desk, never saying a word. She sat down with a thoughtful look. She looked across the room to where Laura sat. A smile appeared on the corner of her lips. She then looked back across the room directly at me. Our eyes met briefly. I put my head down again. I cautiously peered up a second later and could see the knowing grin on her face.

Then a voice piped up to disturb the silence. It was Marius.

"Something funny, Mrs. Woodsmith, that you would like to share?"

At that moment, if the window were open, I would have jumped. Seriously. The fresh snow would have broken my fall.

She got up from her chair and moved out to the front of her desk. By now, most of the class had put their books down to see what the commotion was about.

"You amuse me, Marius. The truth can be so near for some who dare to seek it. So far for those who cannot see."

"What?" he replied in a state of total confusion.

"Exactly. I was reflecting upon a joke a fellow teacher told me earlier today. It remains quite funny thinking about it."

"Why don't you share it with us so we could all get a laugh out of it?" Marius did not enjoy the teasing and was trying hard to turn the tables and claim a victory.

"I would, though I don't think you would get it," she said gleefully just as the bell rang.

Marius, utterly defeated (maybe for the first time I'd ever seen), tapped me on the back with his pen.

"What was *that* all about?"

"I've given up understanding teachers, Marius."

Marius raced out the door, giving Mrs. Woodsmith a stare on the way out. I slowly passed by her with vigor, eager to avoid further scrutiny. I remained ever hopeful Marius's scowl had distracted her enough.

"Have a very nice weekend, Mr. Wells," she said as I was about to pass the doorframe. I didn't even have to see her face.

Her smirk was omnipotent and weaved its way through me.

I turned and glanced at her and muttered a quick soft, "Thank you," and left.

CHAPTER 20

Christmas was always special. Unfortunately, it marched tortoise-paced toward you and ran away faster than a hare. In between, you barely had time to savor the moment. This year was even more special. My heart sang endlessly songs I couldn't recognize and lyrics I couldn't make out. I merely lived in tune with the melody of how they made me feel. The layer of snow outside in the park propagated ever so slowly. There were days when the rink in the park was a steady pattern of hockey amidst the falling snowflakes and shoveling.

Today Mrs. Woodsmith made an announcement. "You are to all prepare a poem by the end of this week." The quiet murmur of submission from the class followed her declaration. "This time, you will not be handing them in but reciting them in class. It will be twenty percent of your semester grade. They can be any length and on any subject. Presentations will take place beginning Friday."

"One tiny detail . . . they have to be original poems."

The groans went off like mortar volleys through the class to only be silenced by the class bell.

Marius was quick to jump to his feet. "Wells, write me a sonnet, please. Not too good, just good enough." He was half joking. If I wrote him a horrible one, I'm pretty sure he would accept it at face value and present it. It certainly would teach him a needed lesson.

"I'll have trouble writing one myself by Friday, let alone writing you one!"

I walked to my locker, opened it, and buried the maniacal grin I had inside. I would be reciting a poem to Laura. An audience of one amongst many. My heart fluttered with both the opportunity and the thought of her listening to my heartfelt thoughts. Whatever I wrote now had to be singularly amazing.

***

The next few nights were sleepless and restless for me. Nothing was good enough. I filled wastebaskets with doomed ink and defective words. I needed to study for a physics test at the same time. I finally closed the textbook around 2 a.m. and went back to my thoughts and my dilemma. I drifted off to sleep with stereo headphones on and record player stylus long since upright and back in its holder.

My night's toil began as the marriage of the lunar glow with the crystal-like snowflakes that evening lit up my room like thousands of fireflies. The words filled my head haphazardly, ricocheting off every wall before calmly settling into place. I couldn't tell if I was asleep or awake. It made no difference to me.

> *It pulls me down from this soft cloud,*
> *dances with me and pulls me tight.*
> *As time nibbles on the playful moon,*

the envious sun belches in a bright orange haze.
Come dawn, our dance, prematurely over,
gravity pulling me from this dream;
Falling farther from your outstretched hands,
the unburnt embers breathe life and pledge together
to defeat gravity and hold you forever.
Their flames fuel my love and serenade a lonely moon,
loyal forever to dreams once too often betrayed.

I wrote the words down on a piece of paper. It wasn't hard for me to memorize them. It was truly a full moon shining through my window that night. A spider had started laying down its silky trail from the top frame of the glass to the bottom. The moonlight shined off this delicate string and glistened before my eyes. I thought of plucking the string to hear the wondrous music trapped within it. I finally slept— and slept well.

I walked to school with a quiet confidence. Along the way, Moony recited to all, whether we cared to listen or not, his forty-eight-stanza poem. Not once but twice. It was a consummate Moony performance. Pure nonsense and pure charm all at once. Marius had obviously done research and had a short poem called "The Blue Wheelbarrow." His word count was about fourteen. From the time Marius told it on the way to school to the version at school, the words changed.

Finally, my silence grew noticeable.

"C'mon, Wellsie. You're holding out," Thomas demanded.

"Guys. I'm not done yet. I'm finishing it at recess. I'll recite it on the way home."

Just then the school bell rang; I was safe, for now.

Time oozed forward and meandered toward English period with insecurity flooding my heart. *My homage had better be beyond just good. But, what if it sucked? Seriously.* I took a long stuttering breath. Slowly but surely, anxiety took over. I saw Janie at her locker a couple of rows down from mine. She was adjusting her hair in the small mirror perched perilously on the top ledge of her locker.

She was usually pretty darn blunt but honest at the worst of times. Better still she was not in my English class. Her ears would be the perfect audience for a poem designed for a young woman.

"Janie! Moony asked me his opinion on a poem he wrote for English today. I desperately need a woman's opinion, okay? I mean, I don't know what to tell him."

"I heard it's an hour long, you serious?" Her hand brushed aside a stray hair from her face as she spoke.

"No, he wrote another one," I said, handing her the fruits of my labor. I prayed she didn't recognize my handwriting.

She read it slowly. Her facial expressions were thoughtful as her eyes squinted, studying the page. She finally looked up with a smirk. "Not my cup of tea. Pretty good, I suppose. Has Moony been drinking? It doesn't sound like him."

"Yeah," I said, laughing. "Thanks. I'll let him know it's good to go. Then again, he may go with the other one he wrote," I said as I desperately tried covering my tracks.

I walked into English class and almost choked on my exaggerated gasps of air and closed my eyes for an instant. Marius had his weighty feet up on the radiator at the back of the class. I could see the overcast sky outside. It was the kind of sky that foretold a winter storm. To my shock and dismay, Laura wasn't there.

I went to my desk and prayed she would walk through the door. It didn't happen.

As Mrs. Woodsmith went through the attendance list, faint hope made a brief cameo appearance. "Ms. Winters."

"She's sick today," responded a female voice on her behalf. I almost thought the thud in my heart would echo throughout the class. I put my head down, hoping my sigh had gone unnoticed.

Damn it. Double damn. I took the paper in my hand with my poem and tucked it neatly in my writing notebook. There was no way I was reading that. Especially since she wouldn't hear it. I thought maybe Mrs. Woodsmith would not call me to read mine and hopefully Laura would be back next class.

Then she went through the list of reciters for that day, and there was my name: fifth. I had maybe twenty minutes to write a new poem. One by one the four students preceding me came and went, during which time I wrote feverishly.

> *The snow, it falls covering*
> *the quiet despair of summer's hope.*
> *Of flowers, long since grown and dead.*
> *Of hope, betrayed without a whimper.*
> *Alas, the tree branch shelters the last squirrel.*
> *It will remain warm, returning with spring.*

I will wait in frozen fascination;
Reborn, when a new hope
preys vengefully upon my tortured soul.

I had just finished when my name echoed across the room.

I don't recall going up or reciting. But I know my eyes never left the white landscape in front of me. It was pretty darn gorgeous.

When I returned to my desk, Moony gave me the thumbs-up sign from his seat and Marius patted me on the shoulder. He leaned over and whispered, "At least you didn't have a hard-on while you were presenting." The highest compliment you would ever get from him.

While the class listened to Moony for a good thirty minutes, I sat with my head down. One more week to go before Christmas break and then I wouldn't see her for two weeks.

I walked home dejectedly that day and sat on a park bench for what seemed like hours, just staring at the footprints that led me there, and watching the soft snow falling and gently filling them in.

I got bitterly sick that weekend, enough to make me miss school on Monday and Tuesday. I assumed Laura had returned and recited her poem while I was absent.

My parents took the opportunity of my being around the house with time on my hands to have me sign off on my college application. It seemed like a lot of paperwork for one school. I was so sick I couldn't care less at that point and didn't know what I was signing. I finally felt like my old self by Friday, the last day before school was out for the holidays.

English class was early that morning. I depressingly looked at Laura as she left class that day to attend her next one. My vision of her would have to keep until early January. I turned to Marius.

"Hockey at the rink? During holidays? I'll bring my shovel."

"I'll be around. I'll bring lots of pucks."

Even that saddened me. We expected it to be our last winter on the outdoor rink together.

I wore my flight jacket all through classes that day. I felt slightly chilled as I walked to my locker for the last time before the new year. I opened it and held my notebook firmly in hands. Pages and pages filled. I clung to it tightly and closed my eyes briefly. One day I would sit back and read what I wrote. Not today and not for a while.

I was about to close my locker and turned my body slightly. Someone was there, right next to me. A bright ember sparked somewhere nurturing a warmth that filled my body. It was like the warm massage of a fever. Instead of feeling weak, my heart pulsated to a gentle beat. I didn't need to see or hear; I knew who it had to be intuitively. My heart whimpered softly like a puppy. I turned and met her eyes briefly and drowned in them. I looked down not wanting to betray my secret.

"Sorry. I didn't mean to creep up on you," Laura said. Her voice caressed and nibbled on my ear.

"No. Not at all. I didn't want you to get hit by, you know . . . the locker."

"I see; I'm okay. I wanted to ask you a favor." Her eyes opened wide. I summoned all my energy and my senses to commit to memory those soulful dark eyes and long lashes.

"Sure," I said, almost fainting. If I had fainted, it would have been a fitting death. The last image being her eyes. Life just does not make things so fundamental.

"It's our last year in high school, and I'm making a memory book. In reality, it's a kind of scrapbook."

"For the school yearbook?"

"No. This yearbook is my own special one. I want to have a keepsake. I know it sounds trivial."

"Not at all." I melted now, serenely and invisibly. *Trivial?* Here I was, holding tons of paper with my obsessive musings.

"I know I missed some of the poem recitals and wanted some for my scrapbook. I mean just a copy. Mrs. Woodsmith suggested yours as one of them. She said it was quite good."

"You spoke to Mrs. Woodsmith?"

"Yes. Mrs. Woodsmith suggested yours. If it's a problem, don't worry. You can keep it. I just want a copy."

"No. Honestly, it is no problem at all. I'm glad she thought it was good." I started shuffling the papers I had. I realized I had stuffed it into my notebook.

"Wow. You take a lot of notes," she said, pointing to my notebook with papers sticking out all over.

"I guess I like to write… maybe too much sometimes," I said, giggling. At that point, I felt totally at ease swimming in an endless ocean filled with calm, warm waters.

She laughed. "You're not the only one."

I finally found the poem and handed it to her.

"The library isn't closed yet. I'll hurry and make a photo-copy and bring it right back to you." Now the smart, logical choice would be to accompany her to the library and steal every second with her possible. Of course, my mind no longer worked in tune with the laws of physics or logic.

"No. Please, you can keep it."

"Seriously. I can't keep it. You probably worked hard at it."

"Trust me. It means a lot that someone would want it. It's yours. Please keep it." I handed the paper over to her, and our fingers gently brushed.

"Thanks so much," she said, staring with her vast dusky eyes right through me and swallowing my soul. She started backing up and as she did, she said: "Merry Christmas—and thanks again."

She slowly moved backward, watching me. No words could come out of my mouth. A million thoughts and images raced through my mind, including how I should give her the original poem that was meant only for her. Finally, as she was about to give up and turn, it came out.

"Merry Christmas, Laura." She smiled, seemingly satisfied with the response, and walked away. I closed my locker, and Marius was beaming, with Moony close behind.

"Talking to girls who keep scrapbooks. Nice. Very nice. Tea and crumpets at four? What is going on with that?"

"She just wanted my poem for her scrapbook. Besides, she reads . . . I am . . . never mind . . . just because she wants my poem."

"Whatever," Marius said, shaking his head.

Moony seemed totally confused as usual and whispered to me. "Why does he think what you did was wrong?"

"Typical Marius. He has something against us book nerds!"

I knew this would stir the pot and create a needed diversion of attention.

Moony fixed a glare on Marius, who watched him in utter amusement. Moony shook his head and waved a finger at him.

"Don't put down kids who read. I read, and I mean a lot!"

"Good lord. Let us not get carried away. Reading. Yeah, okay. As for you, Moony, we all know you are a great shaman, so I *love* the fact you read." He smiled from ear to ear, clearly bemused by Moony's interjection.

Moony, now satisfied, moved along and left the school with us as we headed home for the holidays.

When I finally got to my room that night. The events of the day played on like an endless tape loop. I mused on how to encapsulate the events of the day. There were no more suitable verses ever expressed.

We were together;
I forget the rest.

CHAPTER 21

During the holiday break, I had written furiously and feverishly, going to the cabin in the woods early before meeting Marius and Moony at the rink. In the winter, nobody went there. It was the perfect solitude for a young heart. I would arrive and pry the door open and sit on the bench alone and write. I knew no one would bother me. By the time classes started again, I felt alive and no longer alone.

The school looked decidedly different after Christmas. It had become less of my school and more of my home. I longed to spend every second, minute, and hour in it. I immersed myself fully in each and every subject, whether Laura was in those classes or not. The fact was, I thought of her as always with me and therefore never wanted to let her down. Whatever connection I made with Laura before the holidays kept me warm as the temperature plummeted.

I sat in English class and daydreamed about the two of us. Many times as my name would be called, Mrs. Woodsmith would have to repeat it louder to snap me out of it. Marius took great delight in slapping me with pen, pencil, or ruler to get my attention. No one seemed to care about my flights outside of their world, which I regularly took. I was beaming, and no one could take issue with that.

Time is a merciless foe in our youth. When one is too

complacent, it quickens the pace, and before I realized, the calendar had turned to February. January being a mere icy speed bump. I grasped that merely orbiting my love and being comfortable in stable orbit could not sustain me forever. One day I looked across the room, my eyes gazing upon Laura as she read aloud in class. My heart cried out from a cavern within me and frightened me. It was not a cry which anyone in class could hear. My secret was surely safe. It was a plea from my heart to awaken my brain and spur me into action. My heart continued to sing to an empty concert hall, and now, it demanded more.

The classroom calendar had but one date on it that mattered most in the month of February: Valentine's Day. We spent many classes leading up to the fourteenth reading poems and particularly poems of loves won, loves lost, and loves unrequited. It was a tradition within our school to sell Valentine cards. For two dollars, you could buy a card and send a message, which would be hand-delivered to a classmate's locker. The proceeds went to charity. My opportunity was waiting for me. To ensure the anonymity of the sender, you would be able to buy the cards at the administration office at school, and drop them off in the red "mailbox" near it.

During one lunch hour, Marius pulled me aside in the locker bay. I could see him reach into his jeans and feel his way around. He pulled out a twenty-dollar bill and waved it in front of me. "Kiran, Valentine's Day is coming, as you are aware." The brilliance of Marius was that he would make the obvious ridiculous observation seem as significant as being Newton beaned by an apple.

"Yes. I figured that out. Happens every year around this time by coincidence." I couldn't help but take a shot at him. The opportunities presented themselves so rarely. "Sorry, Marius. I couldn't resist. Yes, of course, Valentine's Day. I take it you're planning to send a card to someone." I motioned with my left hand at the cash in his hand.

"Yes, you catch on pretty quick."

I stood and watched his eyes carefully. My math calculated eighteen dollars in change for a card. However, Marius's eyes were winking at me. He had some master plan up his sleeve and needed my indulgence. "So, what's the catch?"

He reached deeper into his pocket and pulled out another twenty-dollar bill and waved it in front to me. "Get the picture now? I mean, you must have caught on now."

"Oh, brother, Marius. This scheme seems like a doozy. I'm guessing that with forty bucks you're planning to buy a card, flowers, and some chocolates for some girl. It doesn't seem like you to go all out like that."

"Wrong. Wrong and completely wrong."

"Okay, what's going on? If you weren't waving money around, I would've thought I was talking to Moony."

He laughed, enjoying the drama he created. "I thought it would be fun for a few girls to get cards . . . and . . ." He paused, and I now felt my throat constricting, almost knowing what was coming next. I tried to corral quickly this bull that was getting out of control.

"You want to send twenty cards to twenty different girls?! Geez. You're going to actually write twenty cards?" He stared back at me and smiled. My stomach dropped. "Why am I thinking I'm expected to write the cards for you?"

"I'll do the hard part by choosing the girls and addressing them. You have the easy part."

"What easy part?

"What could be more romantic than a poem?"

"Are you serious? I have to write a poem for you."

"Yes. You're good at it. It won't take you very long."

"Girls talk, so it'll look pretty stupid when they all got the same poem from you." I realized how bottomless the hole I dug was the instant the words came out. "You want me to write twenty different poems for you?"

"Yes. Four lines each, not more, not less." He put his arm around my shoulder and gave me a big squeeze. "Just write the poems and I'll decide who gets which."

I thought about it for a second, and the sheer madness of it made me smirk. Each of these girls was going to get a Valentine card from Marius with a different poem. I couldn't wait to see the fan when the shit hit it.

I went home that night and composed twenty of the most innocuous four-line poems of all time. The first two lines were all *Roses are red. Violets are blue.* It never occurred to me how many words rhyme with red and blue.

Marius's project kept me busy. I had forgotten there was the deadline for the Valentine's Day cards. I arrived two days before Valentine's Day to learn there were no more cards available. I missed the deadline for submitting by a day! I stood in front of the administrative counter speechless. I had spent two nights writing out Marius's stupid cards and giving them to him to send as a joke. Here I was with nothing to show for it. My true love would not be getting a card from me.

I strolled to my locker during lunch hour, opened the door, and pulled out my notebook. I read the poem I planned to give to Laura.

> *When I started to crawl,*
> *my body rebelled and tumbled forward.*
> *This love slipped from my lips.*
> *Across my path, it settled.*
> *My heart blew it away*
> *like, fine dust.*
> *Inhaling with a lonesome breath,*
> *to hold until the moment,*
> *when I learn to walk.*
> *Savor, forever the day,*
> *this love to your lips delivered,*
> *sealed with a gentle kiss.*

I closed my locker and in front of me stood Moony. I had no idea how long he was there or if he noticed anything. Moony was not the type to filter his words, so I could tell by his blank stare he was oblivious to my plight.

"Kiran, I just came to see where you were. I didn't see you in the cafeteria. Are you coming for lunch?"

"Yes. I just forgot something in my locker."

"There has been quite a buzz in the school with all this Valentine's Day stuff. Did you send anyone a card, Kiran?"

Moony's eyes widened and a smile permeated across his mouth. Normally, such a question would have been an accusation of sorts. Not with Moony. He was genuinely curious and entirely innocent.

"Well. I did help out someone writing cards and got tired out."

"Ah, yes. Marius told me about his big project. Quite a secret-agent task he gave you."

"What did he tell you about his project?"

"He had you write cards with poems for twenty girls."

"They were from him. He was supposed to sign them."

"He did sign them. But not his name."

My heart dropped, and the air around me seemed to all evaporate at once. "Whose name did he sign?"

"He just signed it from a secret admirer. He thought it would just be more fun for the girls to wonder about who it was and they could imagine it was from someone they genuinely liked. Why? What did you think?"

"Never mind. Marius never ceases to amaze me." I put the poem I created inside a textbook I had in my hands as Moony was speaking.

"You know what would be nice to do instead of just a regular card?"

"What, Moony?" I was more than curious.

"To give someone something personalized." Moony's eyes darted about as though the idea came to him as fortuitously as flies gravitating to a hungry frog.

"You're a wise man, Moony. A true shaman and soothsayer."

"I don't think I can be both. Nevertheless, I appreciate

the compliment."

"Now let's grab some lunch."

We walked to the cafeteria. While my heart embraced in full euphoria the notion of handing Laura the poem on Valentine's Day, my brain sent a gentle reminder notice to my heart.

While my heart was all in, the rest of me was paralyzed in teenage fear.

CHAPTER 22

I paced around my room during the nights preceding Valentine's Day. There was only one way Laura would get a card from me: I would have to deliver it personally and watch her read it in front of me—and pass judgment on my feelings. Her facial expressions would either embrace my heart or cut it into pieces with razor wire.

I sat in the chair in my room, and studied my surroundings. I supposed I could do nothing and let the day pass like any other day, a truly safe option. The feelings inside me would be insulated from ridicule. I could enjoy the day and laugh at the collateral shock from Marius's prank.

I arrived at school the morning of Valentine's Day content, having convinced myself that the safe path was the correct way. I was too scared of the potential response and decided there was plenty of time in the future. Christmas had proved one thing: some moments could come so unexpectedly. *Why risk a disaster now?*

When the five-minute warning bell rang, instead of rushing to class, I lingered at my locker. I leaned my back against it and slithered down until I was sitting on the floor. I pulled the paper out of my textbook and re-read the poem I had authored. I slid my finger along the words and closed my eyes. I entered an ominous cavern in my mind and could feel my heart's agony. My eyes opened and I got up and walked to my first class. English class would be after lunch and any cards addressed to us would be delivered to our lockers during our final period. I had convinced myself that inserting the poem in the locker with others seemed so impersonal. Besides, I wanted to see her face as I handed it to her.

I ambled into English class and took my regular spot. Marius was in an even more jovial mood than usual. It was Valentine's Day and his grand prank would be unfolding over the course of the final period. Twenty terribly written poems would have girls guessing all weekend as to the identity of their secret admirer. My prank on Marius was to write the worst possible poems and have his name associated with them. This poor secret admirer would go down as the worst poet in the history of humanity.

Mrs. Woodsmith was in a playful mood. In the spirit of Valentine's Day, she asked the class to ponder what love means to them. In her usual fashion, she looked around the classroom, hoping to provoke a discussion. She went around the room, throwing grenades at various unarmed students. One by one, my colleagues combusted into flames. Moony sat with hands raised the entire time, in eager anticipation of giving a well-considered response. I could hear Marius fidgeting behind me, waiting to set a match to this tinderbox of a discussion. Words bounced all around me, independent and meaningless until Mrs. Woodsmith said, "Laura, what is your definition of love?"

My soul sailed immediately across the classroom and

pressed itself against her lips to hear the words as soon as they came out. There was a brief silence as she closed her eyes summoning the words from a place within her. "Love elevates one to a higher level of being." The last words fluttered out and danced across the room into my ears. Her eyes opened as the last syllable came out. My heart was paddling in the boundless depths of her eyes.

"Very insightful and words with very deep meaning."

Suddenly Marius erupted in his usual fashion. He poked me from behind and leaned over to whisper to me. "What the fuck is she talking about? Has everyone got the Moony bug?"

I was stunned by Marius's words. Mrs. Woodsmith jumped on Marius's facial expression sensing his disregard for a fellow student. "Marius, you seem confused." She gave Marius a menacing glare and Marius fell back into his seat.

"I just couldn't hear and was asking Mr. Wells."

"Could not hear or not understand?"

"A little of both. I suppose."

She turned back to Laura and smiled at her and in a soft voice said, "Laura, would you kindly elaborate for the other side of the room?"

Laura looked at Mrs. Woodsmith. I could see Laura's lips tremble slightly with a trace of nerves. "Mrs. Woodsmith, I suppose what I mean is that real love elevates you as a person. I'm not sure how to explain it further." Her fingers shook— she seemed to be frustrated by her inability to articulate her thoughts. A brave wind raced through me and swept my heart through the gates of my brain in full rebellion. My hand rose bravely, the only one at this point, as even poor

Moony had given up by now.

"Kiran. Do you have something to add?"

"I believe what Laura means is that when you are really in love, you are consumed with the well-being of the one you love. You would sacrifice yourself and your happiness for theirs without expecting anything in return." I stopped as my heart was palpitating, and I needed air.

"Mr. Wells, you seem to be onto something."

"In doing so, you become a better person because you're giving your soul to someone else. I guess you evolve to another level because of it." The last words came out while my brain was trying to understand what I had just said.

"Ms. Winters, does that make sense to you?"

"Yes. Perfect sense." Laura smiled at Mrs. Woodsmith. I could see her hands no longer trembling. Now, at rest, she looked comfortable on her desk. I was almost waiting for the slap on the shoulder from Marius or his massive shoe against my chair. I wouldn't have felt it.

Mrs. Woodsmith moved on and finally allowed Moony his time (she strategically waited for five minutes to be left).

My eyes diverted to Laura. She glanced over at me as her lips mouthed a "thank you" in my direction. I smiled back and nodded my head, quickly turning to the front. The beast would soon stir behind me. When the bell rang, I reached into my pocket and summoned every ounce of bravery toward my next mission. I would go to Laura's locker and give her the poem after school.

When the last bell rang, the image of Laura trapped my courage from escaping. I went to the locker area, poem in hand. Laura's locker was a few rows over from mine. I waited patiently for the students to dissipate so there would be some semblance of privacy. I had a clear line of sight to her locker when I noticed a card sticking out of it. She pulled the card out and examined it. My eyes looked at the floor as I turned and retreated. She had received a card from someone other than me.

***

For the remainder of February and for much of March, the defeat at the locker bay hounded me. The most romantic day of the year had passed. I had blown it completely. I totally forgot about what happened in English class and the special moment it truly was and became transfixed by her receiving a card from someone else. I grasped in due time that I had let fear claim a clumsy victory.

It was near the end of March when the real comedy of my failure took shape.

One day after class, I took a record to Janie's locker that she had been asking to borrow for weeks. Janie's locker was on the same row as Laura's and well within earshot. I was waiting for Janie to show at her locker when I overheard one of Laura's friends speaking to her. "Did you ever find out who sent you that stupid Valentine's card?"

"Oh, the 'roses are red' one? Yes. I know who sent it. All the girls in English class got one."

"So, who was it?"

"That Marius character."

"Figures. Some people need to get a life."

I laughed inside and slowly hid behind an open locker so they wouldn't see me. My back was turned to them anyhow.

"The worst part was, I was kind of hoping to get one from someone else."

Just as the words came out, Janie appeared. "You brought the record, I see. Great. Thanks! I promise to give it back to you soon. Don't worry."

"I know you will." I smiled and tried to return to the conversation I was overhearing but Laura and her friend were gone.

***

Spring indeed had arrived. I thought I would be ecstatic to learn Laura didn't *really* get a card from someone else. In my room at night, the joy was muted. While my hope grew stronger, I found myself troubled that Laura was disappointed. I could find no peace in that. I thought of this lovely girl who needed help in class that day. Somehow it was my heart that heard her. I looked out the window at the endless sky and thought to myself how elegantly humble love was.

CHAPTER 23

We had stayed late one day after school. It was early April, and, as a delayed April Fool's joke, spring had arrived quite late. Marius had come by my locker and asked me to meet him at the old cabin. He told me he had to tell me something in private. Marius made it clear no one was to accompany me, not even Moony. He claimed he wanted to see if the cabin was still standing after the harsh winter. He had no knowledge of how well used it was over the course of the last few months.

"Hmm . . . Looks like someone has been hanging around here." He looked around in the spirit of an amateur detective.

"Well, I came by once or twice in the winter. Just to check." I had to fess partially up as there were clear footprints in what was now the muddy steps leading to the doorframe.

"Without me?" he said in mock anger. "Did you bring a girl up here with you for once?" He drove his finger into my shoulder, prodding and probing me.

"Yeah. Right." *Only in my mind.*

He sat down on the bench in the cabin and pulled out a paper from his backpack. He looked at it as if for the first time. His eyes grew wide and pulsated with light. I had never seen him smile so enthusiastically.

"What is it?"

Typically, he would have thrown the letter at me. This time, he carefully handed it to me. Before I could read it, he blurted out. "I got in. I got in. They finally accepted me."

I read through the letter quickly. Marius had been one of the few who hadn't received an acceptance letter from Riverside College yet. I had received mine more than a month earlier. While Marius's marks had improved, his past results clearly had been a cause for concern.

My smile grew bigger than his. "Cool. We'll be going to college together."

"Don't forget that freak, Moony. Right? You told me he got his."

"Yes, Moony, too." And of course, Laura, I thought.

Marius pulled out a flask from under his jacket. We had no cups for the occasion. He took a swig and passed it to me. I guzzled without trepidation and took a cavernous gulp.

"Good bourbon," I said.

He leaned over and put his arm around my shoulders and pulled me close. As if exposed by the gesture, he quickly retreated into his persona. He was laughing and, dare I say it, giggling. He had feared rejection, his academic kryptonite. He looked at me and raised the flask to the heavens. The late afternoon light was beginning to recede. The smell of winter's remains soon filled the room.

"This is a special day. A memorable and extraordinary day." He focused on the floor as the last words slipped from his lips and splashed on the moldy wood. "I suppose it's not easy being my friend, right?"

I smirked at him and was shocked by the display of

sincerity and emotion. "No. It's pretty easy once you get used to doing trapeze without a net." I poked him in the arm as he had done to me a million times.

"Thanks for helping me get through. You were the easiest person to copy off of I have ever known." He faced me with a broad smile.

I stared at him with intensity. "Friends would do anything for friends."

"Oh, great. Now you're getting all fucking emotional," Marius said, diving right back into character just as he took one more chug from his drink. The sun descended, giving way to the blackness of the night. It was time to leave, as the cold started slithering up from our boots.

"I'm sure my parents are waiting to have supper with me." I tapped him on the shoulder and put my satchel across my shoulders and left. I turned back to see Marius sitting with a letter in his hand and rereading it again with a wide grin bigger than any sea or ocean I could ever imagine.

I trudged through the muddy fields down past the ice rink that was all boarded up. The spring smells fermented the air with a foul odor unwrapped from the autumn. I finally made it home as the neighborhood succumbed to complete darkness.

I turned the key in the lock and could almost sense the presence on the other side waiting. When the door opened, my parents stood before me. They had never minded me coming home this late or worried about me. The sun had only just gone down and as far as I knew there was no special dinner tonight.

My mom pounced in front of my dad, grabbing my jacket and hanging it up for me.

"Dinner is waiting. Wash up and join us at the table."

This burst of energy seemed so unlike her recent behavior. Usually, she was tired after work and would rest on the couch, watching the news until I arrived. This evening was totally peculiar.

"Uh. Is there something wrong? I'm sorry I'm late."

My dad found his opening and, with a relaxing hand on my shoulder, just smiled at me.

I went to the upstairs bathroom and stared into the mirror. I must have had alcohol on my breath, but they seemed not to notice. They were unusually happy and anxious. I cupped some soapy water in my hands and brought it to my face. I felt a sudden burning in my eyes from the soap, and they quickly started to tear. I hurriedly toweled off as I knew they were waiting for me.

I navigated the stairs with energy only to find them already seated. Everything looked ordinary except the meal was what I termed a "bonus night" menu. Usually, we only ate such big steaks when my dad got his bonus or a raise. I could see the bloody redness still oozing out of these monsters. I scanned the table looking for any clues. Forks, knives, plates, salad bowl, salt and pepper shakers, all appeared to be assembled in orderly fashion.

I noticed "it" as I looked at my place setting. My setting was slightly different from that of my parents. What at first glance appeared to be a napkin was now clearly not. It was an opened envelope. A letter. There was a large logo on the front of it. My heart pretended not to know except I caught on immediately. I moved slowly to my seat and avoided looking at the letter. I reached over for some salt and pepper. Finally, my mom broke the heavy silence.

"Aren't you going to read it?"

"You mean this," I said as I pointed to it. "Hah. I thought it was a napkin. What is it?"

"Read it for yourself," they bellowed in unison, both leaning over their chairs.

I fumbled the paper in my hands and the logo whether upside down or not was unmistakable. "Young College." It was a prestigious college in the south. It was one of "the" colleges.

My eyes still burned from the soap as I read the words printed on the thick stationery.

Dear Mr. Kiran Wells,
It is with great pride that we have accepted your application to attend our school this fall. Please find enclosed information for your freshman year. Please confirm your attendance by returning the enclosed form in the envelope provided. We look forward to seeing you in the autumn.
Yours truly,
Marcus Freeman II
President and Academic Dean
Young College

I took a deep breath. If it had been my last breath on this earth, it would have been memorably tragic and probably ironic. My mom studied my reaction and finally spoke. "Well?"

"It's very impressive, I suppose."

"What do you mean, you suppose? It is undeniably marvelous. You got into Young!"

I could see the look on her face. I didn't even remember applying to Young. Clearly, my parents had. However, it was possible in the hurricane of papers I signed before the holidays, when I was sick, that they may have applied on my behalf and I hadn't realized it.

"It is flattering to be accepted. For sure, I'll treasure and save the letter for my scrapbook." Bull. I didn't even own a scrapbook. A treasure in need of burial is what it was.

My mom rose from her chair and hugged me. She nearly suffocated me. "My son is going to Young." At that moment, sheer terror had established squatter's rights inside me. There was no way my parents could afford this. No way.

"It *is* nice, but I know we can't afford the tuition. It'll be fun to at least look back upon this letter one day. Like a souvenir."

"You don't understand. You are going."

I looked bewildered at her.

"My job! Why I went back to work. It was to save the money for this. You are going, sweetie. Congratulations."

I fell back in my chair. My mom had gone back to work that past two years for me and my tuition. I weakly smiled at her as she leaned toward me and gave me an even larger hug. She knelt down on the floor in front of me and grabbed both my hands pressing them together.

"Son, we love you dearly and are so proud of you. We

thought of this as our gift to you for graduation."

My dad, who had been quiet, reached over for his napkin and brought it to his face. He patted his eyes just as I noticed the tears forming from behind his glasses. He walked over to me and patted me on the head and extended his arm.

"Congratulations, son. No one deserves it more."

I smiled the ugliest smile this world has ever known. Pulled apart were the corners of my mouth. I showed my clenched teeth. Hopefully, this would pass for happiness. I said very little. My parents assumed I was overwhelmed with delight.

The steak bore the brunt of my emotions, as I drew my knife across it and cut it open, allowing its juices to leak freely across my plate. The red meat revealed itself before me, glistening in the kitchen light. I don't remember much about what happened next. My parents did most of the talking. I had become hollow. Their voices rang through me like a bell and vibrated back at them.

I finally looked up at them and excused myself. Claiming to be tired from all the excitement and the events of the day, I hugged them both, thanked them, and went up to my room. I could feel their smiles at my back, tearing through me. They had sacrificed so much for me.

I entered my room and put on my winter pajamas. I took a pen from my desk. My personal notepad remained out of arm's reach. I took the envelope from which the letter came and wrote on it:

I now know.
I had swum in a forbidden dream.
My lonely trust asleep
when the vengeful bird,
through an open window flew.
Circling with appetite
its tired prey,
an innocent string,
dressed as a beautiful worm.
My heart's only stitch,
now forever unraveling away.

I buried my head in the pillow. Whether I sobbed or not throughout the night would never be certain. It didn't matter. The bread was offered to me. A betrayal would surely follow. Friends would do anything for friends.

CHAPTER 24

The end of the school year was a month away. My friends had noticed a change in my demeanor. The grin that they described as my signature characteristic had slowly been replaced by a frown. Even Janie kept her distance and stopped trying to borrow my CDs or ask for cigarettes. Marius had toned down his ritualistic hazing of me.

I suppose everyone sensed I had shut down. I found some off switch inside me and locked it into position. I just passed it off as nerves about final exams, although most knew that was a ridiculous excuse in May.

Many times, I had caught Moony's stare, or, worse, his head tilting on its axis to study me from different angles. He was trying to solve the puzzle of my behavior. He would often tug at my arm during lunch to get my attention. Even he was aware that I stopped listening to anyone. No longer would I glance over to Laura during English class. It was like a horrific magic trick where the disappearing assistant never returns. I knew soon enough Laura would vanish for good. No, not her. I would be the one gone.

We assembled one afternoon for our last gym class. Mr. Platt stood in front of us, clipboard in hand and pen balancing precariously over his right ear. He was in his fifties with thinning gray hair and thick black glasses. Mr. Platt looked like someone who had served active duty long ago and still had the taste of gunpowder in his mouth. There was no doubt he could have killed a platoon with his bare hands. Behind him was the one sight we, or specifically I, was terrified to witness. The rope. The brown twisted rope stretched from the rafters to within a foot off the floor. I got dizzy just looking up. The climax to a year of flexed arm hangs, shuttle runs, and running laps: the dreaded rope climb.

I could see the marks on the rope colored in dark black ink. Each line represented a grade for this test. You started as an F and with each black line you passed, your grade moved up. If you got to the top, you got an A. I was terrified of heights and my best attempt ever was to make it a little more than halfway up for a C. The end of the school year was approaching, and this would be a significant portion of our physical education grade.

The huddled young masses were stretched along the bench as we watched each of our comrades being called forward. We mostly sat with hands clenching, toes tapping nervously, or some additional form of a tick. Athletes, like Marius, made it quite effortlessly. Moony struggled to even lift his legs off the floor and barely went up two feet. Some hands blistered almost to the bone. Legs became entangled in the rope when some tried to hang on for dear life.

My turn came with no ceremony. The gallows awaited. I had hoped the bell would ring before my chance would come. My name was usually near the bottom of the roll. I could thank my dad for that. There was still five minutes or so left before the bell would ring.

I would have to face my inevitable defeat.

I walked slowly to the rope and looked up. It was dizzyingly high. Marius calmly walked over toward me, scratching his leg as he approached. He looked at me and laughed. "Don't look down, buddy," and returned to bench laughing, high-fiving my so-called friends along the way. I heaved myself up a couple of feet and began my ascent. This time was different. I felt anger in me like I had never felt before. By the time I made it up halfway, the blood coursed through me as if heated by an invisible source. My eyes were closed, and I could scarcely hear the courtesy cheers of my classmates. "Don't look down." *Good advice.*

I inched my way up farther and farther. Temptation would be my downfall. I could no longer resist. From across the room, I could see the girls gathering to watch. With mere minutes until the bell rang, they were now watching and waiting at a safe distance. I could feel my strength draining and could picture myself next year at Young College doing the same thing. I gritted my teeth as my arms started trembling.

I was about to slide down and accept my C. My mind quickly established this was satisfactory. But then I looked across the hangar-like room to the girls' side. I noticed one figure in the distance. The long dusky hair was a dead giveaway. It was Laura. She, too, was watching my predicament. It was at that moment that the world began to spin on its axis again. A switch went to the "on" position. I could feel my heart beating to a familiar rhythm. Everyone else vanished. I could only see her and her dark hair and eyes. A lightning bolt shot up my spine and ignited something within me that my insecurities enviously once smothered. She was divine and more so from my vantage point at that moment. I was in the sky, looking at everything from a new perspective. Suddenly fear, logic, and reason gave way to curiosity and something more powerful. A loud chord played upon my spine, vibrating through my frame. I looked up and, with my newly formed strength, moved inch by inch higher.

As I pulled myself up to new heights, I looked across the room over to her. This new strength I found was like wiping the dust off an ancient sarcophagus and rejoicing in the splendor of golden treasure. I moved with purpose, like a rocket launching, and before I knew it, had reached the ceiling. I watched from my observatory and thrust my waist forward and back in a swinging motion. From the top of my kingdom, Laura was all I could see and all I wanted to see. The sun shone through the gym window when a passing cloud danced away. I swung back and forth to the polite applause of my classmates. It was like a cathedral with me perched high atop and swaying like some deafening bell.

A smile, once erased by the stain of my toxic future, found itself on my face. The grin was back. I closed my eyes to savor the feeling, oblivious to Mr. Platt, my classmates, and the ringing bell. Music played in mind and unconsciously, I began singing. Mr. Platt was the first to notice.

"Wells! What are you doing? Come on down. Are you really singing?"

The murmurs of my classmates spread like a wildfire beneath me. I didn't even realize I was singing out loud one of my favorite songs, "Skyway". My eyes shut while I was swaying on the rope, thinking of Laura. I wondered if the same fate awaited me as the unlucky character in the song.

It was at that moment that my hands slipped. I came tumbling down, grasping at the rope along the way to break my fall. I hit the floor with bloodied hands, skin ripping on my way down, and with a sickening thud, I landed heavily on my side. By then, most of the gym had already emptied, except for a few of my classmates and Mr. Platt.

Moony stood trembling in the distance. Too freaked out to come close, though intrigued enough not to leave. I could hear his petrified voice. "Is he dead?" He asked it over and over again nervously. He thought only he could hear. I could. I hoped to hear a reassuring answer from someone. None came as everyone waited to follow Mr. Platt's lead.

"YOU OKAY!?" screamed Mr. Platt, as if commanding me to not be dead.

"Yes, sir, totally fine." I rolled over with a mindless look in my eyes; I could see Mr. Platt's bald head hovering over me, clipboard in tow with a pen.

"Well, good job. An A for you." He looked me over and quickly walked away. I doubted St. Peter ran the gates of heaven so efficiently.

I stayed on the mat and looked up at the rafters from whence I fell. I could feel Marius's Nike shoes kicking me gently in the ribs. "Good job. How the hell did you do it? Man, I would have bet a fortune you wouldn't have gotten halfway."

I started giggling on the floor and then chuckling.

"Geez. What the hell got into you?"

I sat up and looked at him very intently. My eyes inexplicably began tearing. I reached over to Marius and put my hand in a forceful lock position around his neck forcing him to lift me.

"I know what I've got to do. I can never leave . . ." I caught myself as Marius's expression changed in front of me. He was confused and worried, all in one look. His eyes got wide, and his lips took no form, neither smile nor frown.

"I mean, I can never leave home without my gloves again," I said, pointing to my bloodied hands.

"You can be kind of weird sometimes. But you know that already. I think it's spending too much alone time with Moony."

We walked out of the gym together. I looked back across the room to where Laura had stood. She was gone. I knew I couldn't be without her. I drew from her presence a strength and spirit that I never knew I possessed. It lit a flame within me.

When I arrived home, I stared at my parents intently. I needed the courage to tell them. My destiny depended on it. It would not be today perhaps, but it would be sometime. I needed to climb higher now. I felt fear no longer, nor did the straightjacket, woven for me out of that fear, seem permanent anymore. I knew that my love was not to be stored away in a jar nor discarded frivolously.

The courage was within me to tell Laura and sacrifice for that love.

I reacquainted myself with my notebook that night

and aspired to ascend higher and explore what once was beyond my mere reach.

PART 3: REACHING FOR THE MOON
CHAPTER 25
Who Is Rachel?

The door closed quickly and then swung open with equal pace.

"Kiran, you came back! Is everything alright?" I stood speechless, her eyes distracting me as she waited for a response. There was something suddenly familiar in her eyes. The sparkle in them seemed to defy time. She noticed the water trickling down my chin. "Please, come in. You're soaked."

I walked across the threshold slowly. She was wearing faded jeans, a solid red shirt and no shoes. She had on little makeup, and her hair was slightly ruffled. She appeared slightly older than the last time I saw her. In the background, I could see a small rectangular table with books strewn sporadically covering it. She must have been studying.

My intent was to return in anger, hoping to confront some villain who had reached across the continent to shake me from a peaceful existence. Maybe it was the girl on the bus or maybe it was the innocent way that Rachel looked; I couldn't muster any resentment. My emotions ricocheted inside me while entangled in webs and knots. Each feeling fought to extricate itself and command attention.

Before I could say anything, she turned and headed into a room only to emerge with a large blue towel for my use.

I thanked her and took it. As I pat myself down with the towel, I studied her carefully; her eyes stared just as studiously back at me.

"You shaved. For me?" Rachel said with a flirtatious intonation in her laugh. She was desperately trying to put me at ease. The irony was I expected her to be nervous since I was stalking her now. She genuinely seemed content about my return.

"I realized I need to clean up a bit," I said slowly as I glared back at her, mindful of my purpose. "We need to talk," I continued sternly while avoiding the scrutiny of her eyes.

"I see. Typical man. One date already and you're here with the need to talk about stuff," she said with a slightly nervous laugh as if knowing what was coming.

"By all means, sit down." She walked backward and in a flash had stacked all the books on the table to make room for me. I followed her slowly and took my place at the table. She gave me the only chair with a cushion and took the one without it for herself.

I sat down and kept my hands at my side. Rachel leaned forward, staring into my eyes. She grinned ever so hesitantly as if trying to make me comfortable. The expression was disarmingly familiar. I had seen this smile before somewhere, someplace.

Before I could speak, she reached out and grabbed my palms forcefully. For a brief moment, I was frightened, yet the manner in which she held them was gentle and delicate.

I could feel her fingers rubbing my palms as she tilted her head forward.

"You want to know why I was looking for you and why I called you back in California."

Startled by her directness, I pulled my hands back as if they were burning on a hot stove.

"It was you . . . Why?" My eyes betrayed me and looked right into the sea that was hers. Some part of me was still hoping I was wrong about her. "What's going on? Why did you send me the letters? I mean, it was you, you're admitting it?!"

Her body stretched out on the table as she reached out again for my hands. She grabbed them and pulled them back up from my sides. "I don't mean to scare you. Yes, I sent you the newspaper clipping."

"And the other letter?"

"I only sent you the clipping."

My head spun. The more answers I got from her, the more confused and disoriented I felt.

"My landlady spoke to you yesterday. You called me back home and then showed up where I was staying. Whatever could you want with me?"

"I did try to visit you yesterday. I desperately needed to find you."

I looked at her in disbelief. "Why? Who are you? I honestly don't understand any of this." I frowned and shook my head in confusion.

She was calm but seemed to be observing me and my reactions. "I'm not sure where or how to start. Just believe me. I am so glad you came here, *especially* today." Her voice was now somber and low. "At the restaurant, you blacked out. I was going to talk to you then. Until you collapsed."

"Really?"

"Do you know why you blacked out?"

"No. I mean, I don't remember much about it."

"I think I know." She let go of my palms and walked back to the kitchen counter and picked up a newspaper. She flipped page upon page before settling on one. She came back and handed it to me while leaning over my shoulder.

"Do you remember reading a newspaper?"

"Yes. I picked one up at the entrance of the restaurant."

She pointed her finger at an article. "Recognize this?"

My eyes tried to avoid the article as if knowing what was coming.

Finally, they focused on the article she pointed to:

PAULEY HIGH MEMORIAL PLAQUE UNVEILING
Pauley High School will have a special memorial service to pay tribute to the Pauley High School student who passed away 20 years ago. The memorial plaque will be placed at the entrance to the school during a ceremony before this year's convocation in honor of Andrew Kaufter, who drowned in the Pauley River.

While I was reading, I could feel Rachel's arms close around me, squeezing my shoulders tight. She began to whisper in my ear, repeating over and over again, "Kiran. You are going to get through this. Stay focused, think of me, and listen to my voice. I will help you. I need to help you."

She repeated her mantra over and over again. My mind tuned in to her and the image I had of her face. I did not blackout. I kept listening to her voice. Suddenly, an image of her face appeared before me wearing her full smile. A wave of recognition and total panic swept over me knocking me from my seat.

I moved so quickly that I broke Rachel's grip, and she partially tumbled to the side. I raced toward the front entrance to try to escape. Not looking where I was going, I opened the nearest door. The wrong door. What I thought was the front door, in my panic, was the closet at the side.

I suddenly heard Rachel cry out as I flung open the door. "Kiran! Please wait. Don't open that one."

I unlocked the door. Immediately, I realized that it was the wrong door and saw something hanging in the closet amongst Rachel's clothing. There hanging was a long black cloak with a moon logo ever unmistakeable on one side. It was the type of robe worn by a Jesuit priest. It had been years since I had seen one. The memories and pain swam over me. Falling to my knees with my head in hand, I could hear Rachel's footsteps charging behind me as she threw herself onto the floor, tumbling behind me. I could feel her arms around me holding me tightly.

"Kiran. Stay focused and listen to me."

My body combusted into short spasmodic breaths, and her words died in the air before reaching my deaf ears. I didn't know if my eyes were open or closed as visions and faces appeared before me and then disappeared as another took their place. I was trembling violently as she held on tight. I could feel the cold water around me and over my head. I was drowning in the air and her breath.

"It is all coming back to you. Is that it? Did it all just come back to you?"

I nodded slowly, my face bathing in my tears. I had no more strength to run. My past claimed victory as time watched in arrogant triumph. My hands reached out and tugged at the cloak, pulling the moon logo ever closer to me so I could gaze at it. Without looking back, I said in between my heaving breaths, "I remember some of it. Some of it, yes. Who are you?"

She grabbed both shoulders and twisted me around with all her effort. "Look at me. Look into my eyes."

"Why? I don't understand."

"My mom said I had my brother's blue eyes when I was born. Mine changed to green."

I sighed slowly and with such depth, I left little oxygen behind. Inside, I felt a million knives puncturing my existence, stab after stab letting every ounce of air escape. Rachel's eyes were open wide and awaiting mine to probe them to confirm her truth. There was no mistake. Not in the eyes, nor the grin. Moony's eyes never changed to green like Rachel's, but the gleam was identical.

She saw the look of recognition as my eyes were wide and alert. "I'm his sister."

I protested tentatively. "He didn't have a sister. I mean he never said anything."

"He didn't know."

"Oh."

"I can explain."

Guilt riddled my heart. Any selfish thoughts were choked by the grief I felt for her. "I am so sorry. I am forever sorry. It is all my fault. Please, please forgive me."

She gently put her hand on my cheek. "I'm sure you did nothing. You tried to save him."

"Yes, but it was all my fault. Everything." I was now trembling uncontrollably.

Her other hand touched my chin. "I'm here to learn about my brother. I need you now. Please listen to me. My brother . . ."

"I really can't . . ." I stammered. The pain was too severe, and my mind pulled down its hard steel doors in a selfish attempt to numb the pain.

"My brother's dad left our mom right after he was born. My mom couldn't raise him alone. She was too young. She sent him to be raised by her sister. To live here in this town."

I nodded, now listening to the calm of her voice.

"Eventually, my mom moved on, got married, and had me. I never knew I had a brother until about a year ago. My mom finally told me how she had a son who lived with her sister here. When her sister died, she left behind a bunch of things belonging to my brother. That is why I came here. I wanted to learn about my brother."

"It's all because of me that he is gone. He would be here right now if it were not for my selfishness."

"You have to tell me what happened. I want to know about my brother. I know it's painful for you. But I have to know.

It's important to me, and I suspect for you as well."

"This is why you found me?"

"Yes. There is more . . . I mean, yes."

I stared at the cloak as I followed her to the couch. She had me sit right next to her. She held a tight grip on one of my arms. She was genuinely scared of losing me. She gazed deep into my eyes. "Tell me everything."

Suddenly my insides felt like they were being slowly eaten away by carpenter ants, piece by piece of me chewed and discarded. Shavings fell everywhere. If only I could choke on them.

"If you won't do it for me, do it for Moony." My eyes suddenly awoke and went bright at her words. "You loved him, didn't you?"

"Yes. Like a brother."

"Please, then. Do it for him. He would want you to. You need to free yourself of all this. Don't you think he would want that?"

I surveyed the room and peeked back at the closet. The sunlight cast a gentle light through the living room window and bathed Rachel in a light shadow as if she wore her very own cloak.

"Yes. I will try."

She smiled as I sank back into the couch. She let go of my arm and nestled in next to me as I closed my eyes and unwound the film in my mind. I opened my eyes, took a breath, and started from the beginning.

My story started that day in high school when I first met Marius....

CHAPTER 26

Suddenly my story stopped. The film stuck and spun aim-lessly in its projector, just before my graduation. Rachel immediately reached for my hands. I could see the tears in her eyes.

"Why did you stop?"

I could not go beyond that day in gym class. I could only see the film reel spinning with no image projected.

"It's too murky. I'm not sure what happened anymore. My mind is racing. These thoughts are just bouncing around my mind."

She patted me on the back of my hand and then rubbed my right shoulder. "Falling in love is certainly no sin. You shouldn't have been scared or ashamed, especially since you were going to tell her. It seems you concluded you had to. Were you going to give up everything for her? I mean, disappoint your parents?"

I nodded.

She got up and walked to her kitchen. I could see a trickle of a tear start that she didn't want me to see. She came back with water bottles for both of us. She let out a gentle sigh and looked at me. "The girl I spoke to in California was not this girl, was she?"

"No. Just a close friend."

Her eyes were beaming now. "What happened the night you told her?" She asked me with a tone of melancholy. My instincts told me she already knew the answer because she gripped my arm tightly as she asked.

"I'm not sure. It's all still an unfinished jigsaw puzzle in my head."

"Why do you keep saying it's your fault then? Why?"

"I know it is. I feel it inside." I couldn't explain to her that feeling buried inside me. My heart was drowning in quicksand. I started shivering, immersed in an invisible ice shower.

"My goodness, you are so pale." She seemed genuinely worried and felt my forehead.

She looked around the room, thinking. She took an agonizingly long sip of her water bottle as she looked at me with purpose. She reclined back with a somber look in her green eyes I had not seen yet.

"Why don't you take a hot bath and freshen up? We can talk after. I promise I won't peek," she said, trying in vain to release the tension from the room.

I surveyed my surroundings. "Is it okay if I take a bath instead? It tends to calm me."

"By all means do. There are more towels in the closet."

I got up and walked to the bathroom. She followed me and turned on the faucet and adjusted it to a warm temperature.

"We have lots of time to talk now. Take your time and relax."

"I'm not sure I can, but I'll try."

"Ssh . . . a hot bath will calm your nerves. Trust me. I'll even make some tea for you with lemon to warm your insides."

When she finally closed the door behind her, I took off my

clothes and stepped into the warm bath. It was incredibly soothing. I sat and wondered about all that had transpired. *It was Moony's sister who had tracked me down. The poor girl never knew she had a brother. She had his eyes and smile.*

I sat in the tub and closed my eyes. How could I ever tell her what happened? I had seen the jigsaw memories parading in my head like an eternal movie. All I could feel was sadness. She would never forgive me. I was here and Moony was not.

The water surrounding me became hot as I searched for my reflection within it. I tapped the surface and watched the ripples spread out and collide. It was my game to soothe the savage beast within. My eyes focused on the water, searching for something, not knowing what I might find. Slowly, I could see Rachel's face within it, distorted by the waves I created. My eyes opened wide and the face contorted with every ripple as the soft feminine features were slowly morphing. I could then see the face, that innocent young face from the world that once spun around me in bright colors. It was Moony.

My hand reached out to touch his face, and as it did, the image began receding. I leaned forward into the water, and my head moved closer and closer to the water surface as the image slowly disappeared.

"Moony! Moony," I whispered in a suffocated shout. "Grab my hand. Don't go away. I'll save you." The warm inviting water soaked my tired face. I drifted off to a bottomless slumber.

CHAPTER 27

The shock of the bright light of the bathroom is what I awoke to, water purging from my eyes and nose. I was disoriented and could only hear a frantic muffled voice. "Kiran! Speak to me. Breathe!"

"Moony! I need to find Moony. Marius, let me go. Marius, we need to save Moony. Please let me go. Let me go!"

"Moony is gone. Snap out of it. It's me, Rachel. You passed out in the tub."

Through a fog of steam and the crystal lens of the water in my eyes, I could see her leaning over me as she held my head upright. I must have fallen asleep in the water.

"I heard a splash. You almost drowned. Thank heavens I heard it."

I realized I was in the bath completely nude and exposed before her. It seemed unimportant. The pieces of the jigsaw puzzle had been put together. She looked into my eyes as if seeing the pieces of the puzzle assemble before her as well.

"Your memory came back. Tell me what happened. I beg you."

"Promise you won't judge me! I never meant him harm. It was supposed to be a special night for me."

"There is no judgment to fear. I have to promise you."

"You have to?"

Her eyes danced with mine. "You would not be here today if someone didn't save you then. It happened for a reason. There was a reason for you to live. It's time to stop dying."

"There was nothing left after. Nothing."

"That is not true. Take a leap of faith." She started to get up and gave me a gentle pat on the head and ruffled my wet hair. She reached over to the rack and handed me a towel as she got up, never losing sight of me. "Tell me everything about how he died."

"It will never be the same again. Now that you will know."

She looked at me. "Maybe that's a good thing." She slowly backed out of the bathroom.

I toweled off, put on my clothes, and joined her on the couch. I passed a mirror in the hallway. I looked surprisingly different. My eyes were almost a black color now with the white around them devoured.

As I sat down, she looked at me, elbows resting on her knees and head leaning toward me. "What exactly happened that night?"

I closed my eyes and went back in time.

CHAPTER 28
The Final Days of My Youth

It was a beautiful Wednesday morning in June. Our graduation was a day away. The sun announced itself through my
blinds and cast shadows across my room. I hadn't planned
to sleep in originally, yet succumbed after a restless night.
We had our last exam the previous day. Today we had to
ourselves. A final day to enjoy the culmination of our high
school years. Tomorrow morning, we would all meet in the
school auditorium for our grad rehearsal with the formal
grad ceremony after lunch. The graduation dance was scheduled for Friday in the school gym.

I had spent the preceding night staring at the moon. My
eyes locked in unison with it. I may have said a million
prayers that night. Marius had wanted to go to the park and
meet on the hill for a celebratory drink. I told him that could
wait until today. It would make it more special.

The day had gone by quickly and before long it was supper
time. I ate a hearty meal. My parents told me how much
I was going to enjoy attending Young College and not to
worry about being on my own. They would visit me often.
They went on and on about how the girls at Young were
from wonderful families and maybe I would be meet my
future wife there. I listened and listened, hearing nothing.

My father nudged me. "Daydreamer, please pass the bread."

I reached across the table, picked up the bread, and leaned over to hand it to my mom. I would be the Judas soon enough and betray all their dreams. I tried hard to stifle the feelings as I looked at their smiling faces and thought of all they had done for me. I spoke to them quite solemnly. "Um. I'm a bit tired and need to prep something for the grad ceremony tomorrow."

"Prepare something?" my mom asked suspiciously.

"I meant my clothes for the grad dance. I want to pick out what I want to wear."

"So you are going?"

"Yes."

"Without a date, right? I mean just with your friends."

I avoided the answer and nodded both horizontally and vertically to utterly confound her. She wiped her hands on her napkin and semi-smirked as she peeked over at my dad.

"That boy. He seems so out of it sometimes," my mom murmured to my father. I could still hear her.

"It's a big time for him."

I made my way up to my room and opened up my note-book. Instead of writing mere words, I started sketching a picture of Laura. I desperately needed to see her face in front of me. While my drawing skills were awful, I could see her face smiling. My heart raced while my breathing heaved like a boat riding the waves. I felt so alive. If this were all there was to this existence, I would consider my life complete.

Perched on my desk was the letter with the Young logo on it. In some ways, I was grateful—if the acceptance letter had not arrived, who knows when I would be spurred into action. I knew I had to tell Laura how I felt.

I would talk to her at the grad rehearsal. She would be in line next to me, Wells followed by Winters. I would hand her a poem and ask her to the dance. Her answer would decide my future. I sat at my desk and wrote all my thoughts down. Then I took a piece of loose leaf and began writing. I thought it would take hours to write. I was wrong—the words poured easily from my heart through my veins and into my fingers.

> *I shall remember this day,*
> *when a soft, shy light shone.*
> *Searching deep within me*
> *for my darkened, frosted soul;*
> *It nestled against it.*
> *Illuminated with its soft glow,*
> *my awakening heart,*
> *into this new world, born.*
> *Breathe, its first breath.*
> *Nourished by these rays,*
> *I followed the path,*
> *through the lonely tunnels,*
> *to find the source.*
> *Across the once cold, empty walls,*
> *I followed the path*
> *that brought me light.*
> *And into your eyes,*
> *I found a furnace.*

In your presence,
this love was born.
And, in your gaze,
my soul forever warm.

The night seemed eternal. I fought to stay awake to enjoy it before it succumbed to the bright orange sun rising in the east. My last memory was the moon disappearing on the horizon, swallowed by a stronger light.

My parents had already left for work. Alone at home, I wandered from room to room. My parents had provided all this for me, and had scrimped and saved so that I could lead what they thought was a better life.

Meandering into their bedroom, the pictures of me as a child filled most frames. There were also pictures of them when they were younger. Their eyes radiated the heat and energy of a youth filled with promise and potential. In their wedding photo, they stood with arms entwined smiling nervously at the camera. They truly looked happy, like nothing else mattered that day.

My heart slowly cried as I thought about what I was going to tell them. How was I going to betray their hopes and dreams for me? I closed my eyes for a brief instant to fast forward the projector and search my soul for my movie that it was playing. It was an image of Laura and me holding hands on the hill. A still frame in the never-ending movie. My heart grinned, content. I gently closed the door of my parent's room. My destiny seemed clear.

The afternoon crept by slowly. Most of my time was spent

lying on my back, listening to my music collection and day-dreaming. I spent every moment corralling the untamed courage I would need to tell her. The fear of failure—of rejection—was overwhelming. As my music got louder with every drum or guitar solo, so did that sense of dread. *What if this seed that was planted in me months earlier was left to burn and wilt under a hot sun? What if it died from lack of water? What if...?*

I finally got up from my bed and put my notebook into the small brown satchel I carried it in. It was almost supper time. I would be meeting Marius and Moony at the park around 9 p.m. I needed to get out of the house, and nothing would be better than the park on a summer's night.

My parents could sense my anxiety at the supper table. The small talk they attempted was aborted. My dad finally leaned over to me. "Relax. The hard part is done. Our son is graduating."

"Thanks, Dad." I knew I had to set the stage and tone for our future discussion. "I was thinking about Young and me..."

My mother put down the plate she was carrying and quickly came over before I could finish my thought. "Don't worry about Young. We'll help you set up when you get there. They said you could go down in early July and settle in well before school starts."

I avoided her eyes and put my head down. Now was certainly not the time. "Thanks. That makes me feel better." My mom and dad exchanged glances before making small talk about inconsequential local news and gossip. Finally, I pointed to the clock and got up. "I'm heading up to the park with Moony and Marius. I'll be home late. Don't worry. It'll be a tame night."

My dad spoke up. "You may want to take your jacket; it still gets chilly at night, especially with the river."

"I'm fine."

My mom walked over and kissed me on the cheek. "And please be back by midnight and remember the rule: NO DRINKING! You are way too young. Besides, you know how I feel about that Marius fellow."

"Yes, Mom!" I said sheepishly. I calmly grabbed my satchel and slid on my white sneakers and scurried out the door.

***

I arrived at the park as the sun began its descent in the western hemisphere. Time was needed to think and write. I made my way up the hill and into the woods behind to the old cabin. It had graduated in my mind from shack to cabin as I spent more time within it writing. It was my quiet retreat. I sat silently and wrote about what had transpired. I also imagined handing Laura the poem. It was only then that I realized I would have to talk to her.

I leaned back against the wall. I couldn't wait to give her what I wrote the night before. I took out my poem and recited it quietly. Every word captured how I felt. This was the best I could offer. From the one window, I could see the sun retreating across the river, almost appearing to drown in it as it sank on the horizon.

The night would come soon, and so would Marius and

Moony. I debated sharing my action plan with them but decided that Laura needed to be the first to hear my words. Marius and Moony would find out soon enough.

I then realized I had promised them I would bring food and beverages to celebrate this grand occasion. I put my satchel down and stored it in the steel locker in the corner of the room. I would hurry to the local store to get some pop and chips and return before they arrived. *No alcohol tonight.* I knew Marius would be annoyed, but I absolutely needed to be clear-headed that evening.

I quickly ran down the hill and filled a bag with junk food at the local store. I made my way back through the park as the skies darkened. I searched for the moon, yet couldn't find it. When I made my way up the incline of the hill toward the cabin, I noticed colors glowing bright red about a few yards from the cabin. I walked over and discovered a rose bush growing wildly next to a towering maple tree. My mind raced ahead of my heart. Roses would be wonderful to give to Laura tomorrow. *Perfect.* I would stop by tomorrow and pick one.

I walked to the cabin and could see movement through the cabin window. There was someone inside. I hadn't seen anyone else venture this far into the woods, since our encounter with the skinheads, besides maybe Marius. The figure I saw in the window seemed small, and I couldn't quite make it out from afar. I suddenly realized it could only be Moony. *What was he doing there so early?* I went from slow to a quick walk to a full gallop. Upon opening the door, fear leaped into my heart. Moony was sitting on the bench in the corner. There was no doubt what he had in his hands. My notebook and the musings of my wandering heart.

CHAPTER 29

I swung the door open, and all air was vacuumed from my lungs in one breath.

Moony sprang up, startled. The notebook and loose pages he held fell perilously to the ground. He instinctively began scooping them up. I ran over, angry. As I picked up the papers, strewn like shards of my soul, I witnessed his small trembling fingers reaching out to pick up every page, and my mood changed.

"I'm so sorry. I didn't know what it was. I got here early and was bored and started looking around. I thought it looked familiar." He smiled weakly at me, pointing at his old satchel. "These writings are yours?"

"Yes. They're mine, and you're the only one who's ever seen them. How much did you read?"

"Quite a bit. I'm a fast reader." He lowered his head, looking ashamed.

"It's okay, Moony. Better you than Marius."

"So, you're in love?" He looked up at me with wide eyes.

"What do you think?" I laughed, pointing to the notebook he held.

"That look and smile you've had for so long. Now it makes sense."

"No one can know about this, Moony. At least not yet."

He shuffled his feet gently. "I won't say anything, but you shouldn't keep it a secret. These words are all so beautiful and sweet. Let the smoke out or else."

"Or else what, Moony, and how do you know about the smoke?"

"I don't want you to burn up inside."

I took a step back and saw him in a different light. He suddenly seemed ageless and timeless. No longer a young child. He smiled back at me. "You have to tell Laura. I can help." His eyes lit up as he spoke.

"I plan to tell her. Tomorrow. I appreciate the gesture, but I need to do this on my own."

"At least tell me how it goes. I need to know."

"For sure, don't worry. If it goes well, I think you'll know pretty fast," I said, laughing.

"Wow. I wonder what she'll say. I wonder how it'll work out. I mean, what do you want in your soul?"

"I never really thought of it. Funny, I fretted over just telling her; I never thought about it in those terms." I paused, and my mind shifted all the emotions and feelings dancing inside to settle on the most appealing one. I grinned.

"What's important for me is you finding your bliss, your happiness, my friend."

My left foot slowly inched forward sliding across the dirt on the old wood panels, making a clean spot in the middle. "I think if she would smile at me, it would probably be enough. It would be worth it, I think, just for a smile back. Not really any smile. A special one, just for me. My heart would wrap around it and keep my soul warm enough like a good coat."

I grinned childishly at such an idealistic thought. "Moony, am I crazy?"

"Why, no one ever asks me, of all people, if they're crazy. It might be a first." Moony then let out a maniacal laugh.

"Am I wrong in thinking this might be all it takes to be happy?"

"Are you asking me? The answer is so clear," he said, shaking the notebook in his hand. "Have you ever read this?"

"I wrote it all, or have you forgotten?"

"You never read what you wrote?"

"No. I just wrote and wrote and wrote. Truth is, I'm not convinced I want to read it. I think it might be a little immature." My voice trailed off as I reached for the book, but his hands drew it away from my grasp.

"Don't be scared. Your secret is safe with me, for now."

"What do you mean for now?"

"I won't tell; I promise, only you have to let her know. I mean you cannot just let it end. There has to be more; you have to write more. There is more to this story."

My hand trembled as I reached into my pocket. I could see his eyes glistening intently as I slowly unfolded the paper. He studied every fold unraveling as if reading words randomly and trying to piece them all together.

"This is for her. If my tongue betrays me and I take the coward's way, I'll give her this . . . tomorrow. Do you want to read it?" I fumbled the paper in my hands. "Tell me if it sounds right."

"No. Laura should be the one who sees this first." Moony suddenly got up and walked to the one window and looked out as if to answer the call of a nearby bird. I could see his hands open up his cloak slightly as if he were going to preach to the night. All at once, he turned back to me with a wide grin.

"Everything okay, Moony? You look like you've seen a ghost or smoked a bad mushroom as they say in the movies."

His smile got wider and wider. "I don't pray usually. Somehow, something told me it was the right moment to pray, so I walked over to the window and prayed."

"Sorry, if I spooked you with all this, but you're worrying me, you know. Telling her how I feel is not some religious thing. I don't know what'll happen. I guess I'm scared right now. I don't know what will happen. What if it ends right then and there?"

"This is why I said a little prayer. I believe it will work out the way it is supposed to. I have no doubt."

"So, why did you say a prayer if you have no doubt?"

"I can tell *you* have doubt, so some higher power couldn't hurt."

I looked down at the ground, engulfed in a feeling of dread and gloom slowly rising within me. "Please don't tell anyone if it doesn't work out." I reached out and grabbed his arm. "Seriously, I don't need any sympathy."

"Will you go away if this doesn't work out?"

I stretched back and shivered slightly. "I would miss you guys too much; you know that."

"Marius will never forgive you if you leave."

"Moony, he can *never* find out about this. That I've known for so long about maybe leaving here."

Moony looked at me with a quieting grin. He stretched out and reached to put one hand on my shoulder. "I hope you stay with us. No matter what happens, we need you here and you need us. We're friends."

"Always." Moony looked at me sympathetically, his eyes narrowing. I had memorized what I would tell Laura. I practiced it over and over in my mind. It was the easy part. A smile back in exchange for my love.

I suddenly noticed that my pocket seemed light. My wallet was missing. Most importantly, my identification. I assumed I had left it at the store. I had time to get back to the store before it closed. My parents would be completely ticked if they found out I lost my wallet. It wouldn't be the first time. I took the paper with the poem and folded it gently and tucked it away in the notebook. I put everything back in the satchel and handed it to Moony.

"Moony, I just realized I left my wallet back at the store when I got the snacks. Stay here and wait for Marius."

"Can I come with you?"

"No. I'll run and be back right away. Wait here for Marius and watch my bag, please." I pointed to the satchel.

"Sure."

I left the cabin and raced down the hill. Sure enough, my wallet was left on the counter of the store. I slowed my pace as I reached the park and looked up at the top of the hill. Suddenly I saw two figures on the horizon. They were recognizable even in the dim glow of the park lights in the night. It could be Drey and Robbie again. Panic swept over me. Moony was alone—or would be alone until Marius got there.

I ran as fast as I could up the hill, stumbling on the moist grass. When I reached the top, I could see the cabin door open. A slight figure emerged and quickly ran into the woods behind the cabin with two loftier figures following. I remembered my warning to Moony: "Run, Moony. Run!"

My pace quickened with each sound I heard. I could hear them yelling at him.

"What you got in that sack, you freak! Show it to us or we'll take it."

I could see Moony run wildly ahead of them at a pace I'd never seen before. He ran farther into the woods and closer to the river at the bottom of the hill on the other side. The river! The current this time of the year was hazardous, especially if one went out too far. "Please Moony, stay away from the river!" I yelled for them to stop, but in the haunted shadows of the woods, no one dared.

Suddenly, the night was shattered with a splash. I raced with every ounce of energy I had. Drey and Robbie stood frozen at the bottom of the hill near the edge of the river. I could see within the clutches of the water a small figure struggling to fight the current.

Drey and Robbie turned to me, startled. "He just jumped in. We just wanted to know what he had in that bag. Honest. He just jumped in. We didn't touch him."

I ignored them and yelled "Get help!" and in an instant, I was in the water, too.

I swam as fast and as hard as I could. I would raise my head up to see how far ahead he was. I knew there was a point of no return when the current going from east to west would be too strong for even the best swimmer. I could just barely see flailing hands in front of me. I could feel the energy drain from me. The darkness toyed with my vision. My arms were outstretched, hoping to catch him. In desperation, I lunged forward into a powerful current.

I felt a piece of fabric. For a faint second there was hope and then a wave swept across, pushing me to the side and underwater. My hand was empty. Water filled my nose and mouth. The last I could remember was a strong hand grabbing at my collar. My mind went into a wild dream of dizzying colors and spinning wheels.

***

Awakening many weeks later in a hospital bed, a young nurse with pale skin and hazy eyes stood over me with a relieved look. "I'll tell your parents you're awake. They'll be overjoyed." She gently tapped the back of my hands with her fingers almost to a beat.

My parents raced in, both with charcoal-colored circles under their eyes and smiles. They asked me if I had any memories of the accident and I said no.

The vision of the miserable smiles they exchanged burrowed itself forever behind my eyes, forming a noose around my spirit.

CHAPTER 30

Rachel's heavy gasp broke my trance and pushed aside the image of my parents looking down over me. Her large green eyes were moist. She reached over and put her arms around me and hugged me. Feeling unworthy of her sympathy, I catapulted backward. "It was all my fault. Don't you understand? He ran because of me. He ran trying to hide this stupid notebook I carried. All because of me and my wild fantasy."

She looked at me sternly. "He did it because he wanted to do it. He thought you were worth it. Respect that he did it for you, his trusted friend."

"Of course, I respect your brother. The piano I'm carrying on my back is because I let him down. A piano with an elephant on top. He ran because I was a shy little boy with a crush, filled with fear of being exposed."

Her eyes rolled while she shook her head at me. "There's nothing to forgive. You tried to follow your heart. It seems you were far more than a boy with visions of sugar plums." She reached over and gestured at my chest with her index finger and brushed it with the gentlest touch. "You are the one who lost the most that night." A determined look crossed her face. I could sense the mood changing. "Never should a teenager have to go through what you did." She shook her head somberly at me. It was the first sign of weakness I saw in her. The color left her glowing face as disillusionment washed over her. It pained me to see her that way, so much so that I suddenly felt empowered. There truly were noble causes in my world worth the fight. From out of the darkness of the many years, I learned to find light, finally.

The resoluteness returned to her demeanor as she walked across the room to her desk with her books. She opened the drawer and pulled out a letter. I could tell it was old because it was handwritten. She walked across and handed it to me to read.

"No doubt you were wondering why I needed to find and help you. This might explain it." She handed it to me with the slightest inkling of a smile.

My hands treated it as a sacred text. Words from a gentle soul who I missed terribly. The letter was comprised of a looseleaf sheet adorned with faded royal blue ink. The handwriting was distinctly Moony's.

Dear Mom,

I don't know if you've received the other letters I wrote. I hope one day to hear back from you. It's been awhile since I wrote you and, well, I have to tell about my new school and friends.

The school is wonderful. They let me talk when I please, and they seem to like listening to me. I have a new name, "Moony." I've made two wonderful friends. One is named Marius. He's a bit loud and pretends to be tough. He has a good heart, a real warrior, and he is my protector. He's a lot smarter than he acts. My other friend is Kiran. He is quite unique, although I worry about him. He's the first person I met who accepted me. He's like my big brother. I think he's in love. I can tell these things.

Just the other night, when the moon was shining brightly. We danced outside in the park. It felt like we were dancing with the moon. It was funny because I think Marius drank something that made him sick.

I'll try writing more next time. Please let me know if you get this.

Love,

Andrew (Moony)

I lifted my head up to see her face in front of me. Before I could even ask, she spoke. "Before my mom told me about Moony, I always suspected something—though was never sure. I moved here as soon as my mom told me. My aunt left behind a box of his things, including a bunch of letters."

"The letters?"

"He used to write to our mom, although he had no idea where she was. My aunt didn't even know where her sister was. I presume she just pretended to send them and left them in a box."

"And you decided to stay here and go to school here?"

"Yes. After finally finding out about my aunt, I came here and found the letters he wrote and the cloak. They found the cloak but never his body."

"I didn't know that. I am so sorry for your loss. To have a brother and not know it and then find out that he died long ago is devastating I would imagine."

She looked at me and smiled. "It was hard, but there's also a positive side. Did you read the letter?" She made a gesture with the letter she was holding before reaching over to grasp my hand.

I realized what she was talking about just as she started to explain. It was my first moment of epiphany in what seemed like ages.

"Moony considered you his brother. I can always use a big brother. Deal?"

"Anything for Moony. He taught me so much in his way. I am forever his apprentice. He would appreciate me saying that." I hesitated to think carefully of this unfolding tale. "So, you sought me out because of this."

"Yes. I was going to save up enough money and find you out west if you didn't come here!"

"Why the mystery? I mean . . ." I thought about it and realized I knew the answer.

"If you knew about me, you would never have returned. Plus I was scared how you would react, especially you being so far away."

"If you went looking for me, you must have also been looking for . . ." My eyebrows raised at the thought, but she stampeded ahead of my tongue.

"Marius. Yes, I want to find him, too."

"I take it you haven't."

She got up and began pacing in front of me. She appeared nervous and uncertain of herself. "Marius, simply put, has disappeared. I mean, I thought I found him, but then he vanished.

"Around the time I found out where you lived and sent you the letter, I thought I had located him. Your friend Marius stayed in town and graduated college here. He joined the military and served all over the world. He saw combat. Upon his discharge, his mental condition deteriorated."

"Is he alive?!" My mind was racing and pulse vibrating.

"He started showing symptoms of post-traumatic stress. He came back here for treatment in a hospital. He began drinking heavily and behaving erratically soon after."

"Where is he?"

"He was in a rehabilitation clinic. The day I went to see him was the day he disappeared. He hasn't been heard from since."

"He probably ran away when he heard you were coming."

"I didn't tell him who I was or anything like that."

"Marius was always sharp. How long ago was this?"

"A couple of weeks ago. The treatment center thinks he's probably living on the streets." She gave a sorrowful sigh. "I have walked around these streets whenever I have a chance. I have no idea what he looks like or where he might be. I even tried your old high school. No one has heard from him."

I looked at her and feigned control and confidence. "I'll find him, one way or another."

"Kiran, you need my help. After everything you have gone through, there is no way you should be doing this. This is too dangerous for you. You need to focus on positive things like . . ."

I cut through her logic. "Like helping Marius. Moony would want me to do this."

She shook her head. "No. You can't. I can't let you. Live your life now, please."

"I can't unless I help him. I know he's the one who saved me that night. I can still feel those damn monster-large hands on my collar. It was him. I can't move on until I help him."

She looked at me and could see my face contort into serious thought. "I have a hunch you know where Marius might be! You've seen him?"

"I hope I'm right. We may not have much time."

"The anniversary date. Might he do something?"

"Yes. I bet he came back, like I did. Probably like me, he has no idea what he seeks other than . . ." I stopped and hesitated with the words. "Looking to be free of the suffering within."

She thought for a minute. I could see the understanding dawn on her face. "When will you go looking for him?"

"At night, if he is where I think he is, he'll need a place to sleep, and this is the place."

"Can I come with you?"

"No. You might totally set him off. Your brother would get under his skin pretty often. I can only imagine you would too...."

She motioned to the kitchen table. "At least, stay with me and eat something until you go looking. It's been a long day. I would like to know more about my brother."

I smiled at her. "Sure. I have tons of stories." We both shared a meal while I told her what I could remember about her brother. We both distracted ourselves from what lay ahead. As I shifted my legs under the kitchen table, I could feel the paper in my pocket. The second letter that was sent to me.

I sat back and thought. *Rachel had said that she only sent me the news clipping, but then who sent me the letter?* There was a heavy silence between us. I pierced it with a question. "Your aunt didn't leave behind Moony's, um, I mean, my satchel? I mean was it ever found? Have you seen it?"

"If you're wondering if I have it, I don't."

"That means that it must be Marius. He was there that night. That might explain it."

"Kiran, why does finding this satchel mean so much to you? The notebook and stuff?"

I didn't answer, so she got up and walked to the fridge and came back with some homemade honey cake. She continued to be silent, thinking and assessing her next words, I was sure.

"What matters is you're here now. Do know that. There are maybe some things that you can never find again." She paused. "There are also things that were always there and never went away."

I heard her but pretended that her words didn't break the surface of my thought. I saw the moon slowly appearing as the bright haze of the sun dissipated. "I need to go. I have to find Marius."

"Do you have a phone to call me? I need to know you are okay." She was genuinely worried.

It seemed like ancient times when I walked away and set fire to my career. For almost two decades I had been able to play a part that not even the finest thespians could pull off. I managed to forget everything about myself and thrive in a foreign world. It was about my life. I was finally playing myself. "No. I'll be fine." I could see her worry. "Look, I promise to come back here by midnight. If I'm not back, this is where I'll be." I grabbed a notepad on her desk and scribbled "Old cabin at park" with directions on how to get there from her house.

"Does this place still exist?"

"I saw it on the bus ride over here."

I walked into her hallway. She moved in front of me. "Since you're my only link to my brother, do take care of yourself."

"I will."

She reached for my arm as I walked toward the door. When I turned back, she looked at me worriedly.

"I need you to come back. I haven't told you everything."

"I sort of guessed that. One way or another, I will be back."

CHAPTER 31

Moony's Wish

When I walked down the street toward the park, I turned back and saw her in the doorway. She waved at me like a nervous mom on her child's first day at school. I put my head down as I walked. *Moony's sister...!* The Marius I once knew would get quite a kick out of that.

Through the park and up the hill, my senses were overcome with the aroma and colors of nature in full bloom. It appeared recently landscaped and well maintained since the old days. The grass crunched beneath my feet. The trees planted in the days of yore were now fully grown. Some pear trees and some apple. The birds chirped, signaling the appearance of this familiar stranger in their midst. I squinted to see my old high school in the distance. The muffled noise of the kids in the school was audible in the distance. It must be grad night for I could almost hear the beat of the music. After midnight, this park would be swarming with partying teens. If Marius was here, I needed to find him fast. I hoped I was terribly wrong. Not finding him terrorized me much more.

I reached the top of the hill and could see the cabin as it always stood nestled within the woods, barely visible now as the surrounding trees had grown overtaking it. The fading light of the sun shone on the windows making them tinted in appearance. I couldn't tell if there were any signs of life within. I walked gingerly toward the cabin, ever mindful that whatever I found was likely to be different than expectations.

Approaching the door, I could hear Rachel's words of wanting to tell me more and how I needed to return. I discounted it to some game of hers to ensure I would be careful.

The forest surrounding the cabin was bright green and the ripples of the leaves spread sweet sounds into my ears. The insects and birds darted from branch to branch creating a natural symphony. I took in the surroundings. *How time has stood still on this hill...!* Such was nature's way, immutable, unchangeable, and self-sustaining. Moony, Marius, nor I could lay no claim to immortality here. We were very much the pawns of board games we played as children. We were moved around by the unseen hand of fate and, when it was all done, placed into a box for the next game whenever that time would come.

I heard a ruffle of a nearby bush against the hard, aged bark of a tree. There was no animal near, so the cunning hand of the wind had jostled it to attract my attention. My eyes fixed on the bush. It was a beautiful rose bush with a single solitary flower in full bloom. I walked over and humbly surveyed it, remembering the last time I had encountered the same rose bush.

I turned to the cabin. I could hear a faint breathing sound inside as well as the shuffle of heavy feet. Marius and his construction boots! It was a fidgeting sound, a pacing sound. I chose not to open the door suddenly, not knowing what form the confrontation might take. Marius had always been physically bigger and stronger and took great glory in reminding me of that in our youth.

I wasn't sure what fate had in store on the other side. I thought about what Rachel had said. Marius had seen and lived in so many shadows over the years while I roamed sunny beaches and corporate halls of tall skyscrapers. He lived amongst those whose life was a fragile existence. He devoted his life to service and risked it daily. Here he was alone and trapped like a wounded bear. *What could I ever do or say?* He had saved me. His reward was my betrayal.

My parents turned away all visitors during my convalescence. In many ways, they brought me to my forgotten shack in the wilderness. I couldn't blame them. They did try to save me in their way. I'm the one who chose to stay hidden and who chose not to remember. Deep down inside, I knew that I was the one, an angry, petulant child, who threw the puzzle pieces haphazardly into the air. Each piece a memory that somehow I hoped could never be assembled whole again. I leaned slightly on the door, bracing myself and realizing I was no longer a victim.

I knocked on the door, like a mail carrier with a parcel too big for the mailbox. I could hear the instantaneous movement of feet across the floor. Someone was taking a position inside. I knocked again and this time a voice bellowed. "Who's there?" The voice was raspy and was followed by a series of spastic coughs.

"Marius. Is that you?" I realized the stupidity of the question as soon as the words dribbled out. More silence followed.

I could almost feel the fuel pouring over his burning soul as he heard my voice.

"Marius. Can I come in?" Again, there was silence. The silence was thick. I had no choice. I opened the door slightly with my right hand and used it to screen me from his vision. Through the open crack, a figure went from a ghostly apparition to a battered down soul.

Dressed in a tattered black T-shirt and torn blue jeans stood a figure. His face was buried beneath a thick brown beard. His hair was dirty brown with what seemed like wisps of gray. His hair was unkempt. His eyes were like coals now. I could see cuts and scrapes around his face. My eyes told me what I needed to know. It was indeed Marius. I could sense his presence long before my eyes confirmed it.

Marius started toward the door very deliberately. I couldn't see his hands or if he had a weapon with him. He began to look around very tentatively. He suddenly turned to the crack in the door and caught my scrutiny. He took a step back, disbelief filling his eyes. His lips seemed to curl into a sneer. Suddenly he sprung toward the door and through the frame. I had forgotten how quick and athletic he could be. Within a split second, he was behind me. Age had slowed him enough that I quickly moved to the side to face him as he turned.

"What were you trying to do?" I said, nervously trying to make light of the situation.

"Jesus Christ. The Savior has indeed returned," he said mockingly. His hands grabbed onto the lapel of my shirt drawing me close. The whiff of cheap alcohol made me cough. "Did they make a big feast in town for you? Slaughter the finest pig or cow or both? The conquering hero is returning!" He pointed his fingers at me, alternating between them all.

"Marius, I'm here to explain. I need to speak to you."

"Speak to me. Now! Incredible. I don't need your help anymore. Those days are over."

"Marius. I know you saved me once. I know it was you. I wouldn't be here if it weren't for you."

He slowly backed off and retreated into the cabin. I followed him. I could see the crumbs of food, parts of sandwiches, and could smell the odor of staleness and rot. I saw the bench and a makeshift blanket on it. In the corner on the floor were bottles with no labels. I looked for needles and pill containers. Fortunately, I didn't find any.

He went to his wooden bed and turned to me.

"Why are you suddenly here, after these godforsaken years?"

His question deflated me. "So you didn't send me the letter?"

"What fuckin' letter? You disappeared better than Houdini. Hiding from us. Why would I try to find you? If anyone wrote letters, it was you. Always scribbling in front of me. You wrote crap, not me."

"I don't know where to start or what to tell you. It was all so wrong what happened. I lost someone I cared about."

"So did I. And someone betrayed me." He said it menacingly and aimed his fingers right at me. I could see the pain bleed from his eyes. It crushed me to see him like this.

"I know now I should have found you years ago. I was

too scared."

"Found me. You lied to me. Friends would do anything for friends, right!" He stepped toward me and pushed me on the shoulder with both hands. I kept my balance. "You remember. You told me that. You would have broken Moony's heart if he didn't drown."

"I decided to stay here and go to school with you. Believe me! Moony knew it. He figured it out that night."

"When were you going to tell me? Before or after the funeral?"

"I was in a coma. My parents told me nothing, Marius. Nothing. When I awoke, I had no memory of what happened." I was suddenly annoyed for some reason and moving toward him. He seemed surprised with the change in my demeanor. "I couldn't remember." I turned my head away from him as the unspeakable truth slid across my tongue only to retreat into my throat and back to the cave from whence it came. "It was so long ago."

"I went to visit. Your parents turned me away. Time and time again. They told me I was trouble."

"I don't know what to say. They were wrong."

"They're the ones who told me you were going south to school. Not you. Them!"

"I closed my mind to everything and every memory." I tried to sit on the bench next to him. He moved his leg, leaving no room.

"You never tried to find me or contact me."

"I shut myself off to everything that made me happy, Marius. It was my only way to survive it. To live with myself,

I needed to hurt myself."

"Survive?" He sounded confused.

"Moony died because of me."

He looked at me. The room grew darker as the last rays of the sun splattered defiantly upon the old wood planks.

"He died because he was scared of those idiots. Don't think too highly of yourself. It had nothing to do with you."

"No, Marius. He was trying to hide something from them. It had everything to do with me. Everything."

"What would Moony have to hide?"

"Moony found my book. It was my journal. Everything that happened that last year: I kept notes with stories, poems, dreams, and hopes. He didn't want them to get it, so they chased him. I don't know why he did that. I mean, he jumped in. He was so scared, he jumped in!" I circled Marius as I spoke. I finally settled in front of him. "How could I ever face you or anyone or even *remember* that he died because of my words." I was tearing now, witnessing Marius's face changing and contorting. He started trembling.

"Marius, I wanted to stay in school with you and Moony. I wanted us to be together. I honestly did. After what happened, I wasn't worthy. I was scared and ran as far away as I could, both physically and mentally."

He was undoubtedly shaking. I thought it might be some withdrawal from whatever he had drunk. His head bent forward and his head tilted to the side. His two large hands rested firmly on his kneecaps and squeezed them.

"You do remember, Kiran. A long time ago. I told the teacher that the world sucked. Why waste words? Why waste years? It's all just shadows cast by a vindictive light. I have been places, buddy. Many places, and I was right. There is hatred, anger, despair, and desperation everywhere and death. Geez, Kiran. We laughed at nukes. If only it were that easy. Instead, we got no nukes. We ran around chasing breadcrumbs. No treasure; only a trap at the end of the trail. Moony died. You even see it now, don't you?" His body tensed up, his teeth clenching. "If they could do that to him. *Him,* of all people! Imagine what's in store for us. Life. We survived that night only to suffer longer. You and I, a far worse fate. I guess you see it now, too." He paused and squeezed his knees again to the rhythm of his breathing. His hands clenched.

"No. I've been dead for too long. There is more to it. There has to be more. Please . . ." Suddenly Marius leaped at me, and his forearms struck the side of my face, glancing violently off my nose as if catapulted by some supernatural force. I could feel the blood slalom down my cheek and into my mouth. My eyes watered as I dropped to the floor. He was behind me in a flash and racing into the woods. I quickly gained my footing as the droplets trickled onto the ground. I ran out the door and shouted, "Stop. Don't do it. Please stop."

"There is still one way to be with Moony!" he yelled as he turned one last time and raced into the forest. "They will make worm's meat of me now." He roared as he ran into the woods.

I summoned every ounce of energy and gave chase. Blood poured from my nose, and the stinging pain half-blinded me. He got to the top of the hill and briefly disappeared from my sight as he began his descent. I knew it was seconds before I would hear that horrific sound of his body against the water.

"Are you joining me this time?" I could hear him yell as he ran in front, provoking me.

I threw myself down the hill and rolled down when I listened to the splash. I was seconds behind. Even in his weakened state, he was strong, but he was swimming toward the current. I knew I had a little time before he would be too far gone. He stopped swimming to look back at me as I cried out. "You can't do this. Not now." My nighttime swimming proved its worth as I caught up to him and grabbed on. He suddenly kicked his feet and continued dragging me with him, visibly surprised by my show of athleticism.

"You can quit anytime."

"I'm not abandoning you, Marius; we are leaving this river together. Someone needs to see you. Trust me."

"Who?"

"Moony's sister. We're all she has to tell her about her brother. Have an ounce of faith. She brought me back here. She needs you, Marius. She's been looking for you."

He laughed as he kicked harder, trying to pry himself free of my grip. "Right. Nice try."

Anger swept up over me at that instance. Or, at least, I thought it was anger, though it was something clearly stronger than anger. It gave me strength to grab onto him by the collar.

"You never let anyone beat you. Never. Why now? All the crap in this world does exist, and it wants to drown us. I'm not giving up. I am not going to let it beat us. You have to join me and swim!"

He seemed startled by my plea, although in defiance he kicked again with his legs.

"Marius, I am not letting go. I'm not. You're going to have to kill me." He seemed unsettled by my sudden display of conviction and the strength that now percolated to a boil before him.

"So be it."

"You can't do this to me, Marius." My breath was heaving now as my strength was slowly dissipating. "I wrote the notebook because I was in love. I was going to tell her."

He stopped kicking and looked at me, confused. The fury dissipated from his brow. He listened attentively. My arms were aching and weak. The waves lashed out at me. I clung to Marius and gripped him hard. I closed my eyes to summon whatever strength I had left. Suddenly I found myself high above the river and could see the endless water. I was climbing a tree that extended to clouds. I saw in the distance a figure standing at the shore. Her eyes shone along the surface of the water and met mine. I opened my eyes and pressed my mouth toward Marius's ear.

"You have to let me tell her. You cannot take that away from me. I won't let you. She must know. I beg you." I gripped him as hard as I could. I knew I had no more strength. The resolve in my words shocked me as the words did themselves. My arms started going limp and my legs began aching. Water started filling my nose as the waves rocked me in their arms. I slowly lost my grip on Marius when suddenly, as I looked into Marius's face, I saw pure fire in his eyes. The coals smoldered within his furnace. There was a kick and then another. This time, it was in the opposite direction. I could feel Marius holding me now and keeping me up. His voice was hoarse and almost breathless.

He yelled in my ear. "*You will stay!* No matter what?"

"Yes."

He propelled me to safety. When we reached it, we both fell onto the rocky shore. We staggered up onto the grass to safety. We lay on the lawn in silence, shoulder to shoulder, staring at the charcoal-colored sky.

He then leaned over and punched me on the shoulder. "Are you alive?"

"Wide awake," I whispered not to him but to the sky.

"So, who is she?"

"Laura Winters," I said.

"Really. Wow. I knew it all along." He burst into laughter and rolled to his side and then sat up next to me. I could see his teeth chewing his lip, suddenly nervous like I had never seen before, and then he lifted his head and stared straight ahead. It was as though endless pools of data were flowing into him and he was processing them all at once.

"You good?"

His teeth bit harder and as he opened his mouth I could see the blood from the indentation he had made on his lip. He licked off the blood with his tongue. He looked at me with displeasure.

"You could have told me. Back then. I could have helped you." He shook his head. "I told you everything."

I dug my elbows into the ground and pushed myself up

to be at his level. It was now, after all these years, that I realized how much I profoundly hurt him. I wiped the last remnants of blood that caked my mouth with my sleeve and looked intently at him.

"Honest to God. I could never explain how I felt back then. Not even to you."

"I guess you figured I would make fun of you?"

"Yes. I didn't think you would understand about me being in love. I figured you would see it as a childish fantasy."

He closed his eyes briefly before a small smirk crept along the lines of his mouth. "I'm sure I would have teased you. I also would have been happy for you and maybe even jealous."

"Jealous?" My ears perked up. Marius, jealous of me!

"Is it so hard to believe? You think I've ever been in love? You think it's that easy?"

"I just assumed with all those girls you knew .. . ."

He looked down, realizing he had opened the door to a place hidden miles within a dark forest. His eyes shifted up and took a peek at me before settling back down. I had found his kryptonite.

"Understand this, I did not leave for anything better. Trust me. Staying would have been better. Not running. Not forgetting. Staying and not quitting."

"Your coma cost you your memory. All this time?" He looked at me sympathetically.

I sighed nervously. My sinister secret finally drifted up from inside the cavern mixed with dust and rust bits. The taste of the river that filled my lungs brought the debris finally to the surface. "No. I never forgot. I'm the one who closed the light. I destroyed every bulb and worshiped the darkness." I fell back slightly with my revelation. "Everything was my choice." I put my head down and rested it on my palms. I did not cry. Dead souls do not shed tears and choosing to forget gave me no entitlement to sorrow or forgiveness.

"Kiran, there are things I've seen . . . I never realized how depraved people could be. I wish I could forget. I never had the strength to lock away all those visions in a prison with no keys."

"No. Marius. I don't think you understand. I stopped living that day or part of me stopped. It takes a braver man to face this world than build a fortress to keep it out."

"Don't kid yourself, buddy. I'm not well. I honestly am not. I have nightmares. I see strange things. Sometimes I need a drink. Sometimes too many."

"I'm staying to help you. I promise you that. I'll do whatever it takes to help you. I promise I'm not leaving this time."

He looked at me, ignoring my pledge. "So, you never told Laura?"

I shook my head. "No."

"That is pretty stupid," he said and burst out into a broad grin, ruffling my hair. "I guess you needed me after all."

I smiled and looked at him as I reshuffled my hair. "I'm not sure how I would find her . . ." Marius leaned over and closed my mouth with his wet palm.

"Shh . . . Tell me about Moony's sister. You were joking, right?"

"I'm not making that one up!"

"Seriously?"

"I think you could use a good meal and a hot shower. She would be pretty excited to meet you."

"You're serious."

"Like I came all this way to pull a fast one on you."

His expression slowly changed. His wet hair and beard betrayed a scared little boy. "Kiran, I won't blame you if you don't stay. I have a lot of shit I need to deal with."

"That is why I'm staying. Friends would do anything for friends."

He sat up on the grass with his knees up closer to his chest and looked at the stars. "What you said. I don't want you to stay for me. You have to stay for her sake. What you said about being in love. That's why I swam back. I want to know what it's like one day to find it. Like if you could, I guess I have some hope!"

"What? Look who you're talking to. The king of all daydreamers."

"But maybe you can tell me what it feels like. The whole love concept and all of that good stuff." He slowly smiled and looked at me, hope shining in his eyes.

"Oh, brother, Marius. If you think you'll learn from watching me, good luck with that."

He looked at the stars and coughed. "That bugger up there. He has us playing around in his dream now. You think he's happy? The two of us here. Wondering about him."

I slowly stood up and looked down at him. "Get up, Marius. There's someone you need to meet. That would make him happy." We walked back as I told him about Moony's letter and his sister.

Marius stopped suddenly on the side of the hill. He pointed over to the rose bush by a tree. He sauntered over to it and arrogantly reached down, picking up the one rose that had flowered and took it in his hands triumphantly.

"Once a ladies' man. Always a ladies' man, eh?" I joked.

"There's only one lady I ever made a promise to—a long time ago," Marius confessed.

"Only one promise and to one lady?"

"Yes. It involves you."

I raised my eyebrows at him, wondering what he was talking about. "Go on."

Marius stopped walking and put his hand on my shoulder. "I promised her that if you survived that night, you would tell the story."

"The story?"

"Yes, in your own notebook-writing way."

"Sure, anything else?"

"Yeah, I want it to have a happy ending." Marius grinned. "I'm sure of it."

"We'll see." I looked at him, puzzled, and continued walking.

"At least I'm not asking you to cheat."

We both laughed as we walked under the bright rays of the moon.

CHAPTER 32

A Dance for Moony

Later that night, after introducing Marius to Rachel, I went back to the park. I needed to be alone with my thoughts. I still didn't know who sent me the letter with the poem or where my satchel and teenage writings were. I was hoping to read them again; hoping that it would remind me of what it was like to be alive.

I could hear some of the kids in the park as I approached, while they celebrated their special night. The dance was over, and they were milling about outside the high school. I walked by them on my way to the riverbank. Couples holding hands were scattered everywhere. I felt a cool breeze coming from the river.

Amongst all these teenagers enjoying their youth, I was a solitary figure again. I looked up at the night sky and felt the welcoming warmth of the moonlight on my cheek. I could hear that voice again as I reached the side of the hill by the river. It was Moony's voice asking if there would be dancing tonight. I smiled at myself and the comfort of hearing his voice.

I sat on the bank of the river. It was eerily calm tonight. The moonlight cast reflections on the waters splashing light into my tired eyes. I almost had to blink. The river suddenly revealed itself as an ageless and restful place. I believed my purpose was fulfilled. Marius had needed me here just as much as I needed him. I had all of the time in the world and sensed he would need every second of it.

Soft footsteps, coming across and down the hill, grew louder with each thought. Reaching into my jacket that I held in my hands, I looked back at the stars as I unfurled the paper I had carefully hidden in the inside pocket. *Who had sent me this?*

To my horror, the page was splattered in a quantum dance of blue ink. If I had been in a psychiatrist's office, it would easily pass for two giraffes holding hands. It was not. My foray into the river with Marius blurred the ink, leaving behind a blue smudge. The poem vanished forever now, leaving me with memories and an abandoned promise. I shut my eyes in quiet thought. I tried to imagine who it was closing in on me. I could feel the breeze of the river brush against my cheek and the paper in my hand swoop up and out of my reach, glancing off my right eye and away. The figure sat next to me quietly as I continued to stare at the river, gently rubbing my eye.

"It's been a long time, Kiran. You know, I still have some CDs of yours, if you want them back. I stopped smoking years ago, too, so I won't ask you for a cigarette."

Without looking at her, I grinned. My head looked down at the ground. It was a voice that quietly drifted in from the faraway lands of my childhood. A most welcome friend.

"Hi, Janie," I said. I turned to face her and to confirm my instincts. Her head tilted toward me to meet mine at the same angle. I hadn't seen Janie since the last days of high school. Her eyes were a darker blue than I remembered. She was wearing a black shawl with a white blouse and long skirt. She wore flats. Her hair was delightfully long, blonde, and tied at the back with a blue ribbon. Gone were the piercings of a rebellious youth. Sitting beside me now was a stunning flower.

She punched me on the shoulder and reached over and grabbed my chin to study my face. "Your eye did recover quite nicely. Never looked better."

"I see you grew your hair out again. Nice touch with the blue ribbon," I said, motioning to the back of her head. "You want to tempt me again. Got to get the left eye, right? Won't happen, my dad taught me!" I laughed at my failed attempt at false anger.

She smiled back with no response. I could almost see her lips moving, practicing her next words. Finally, her eyes looked out at the river and back to me. "I'm sorry, Kiran. I know you were hoping it would be someone else sneaking up on you."

I followed her eyes and looked at the ground and the satchel that she delicately placed in front of me.

"I can only assume you sent me the letter and had the satchel and everything?"

"Don't be angry with me."

"How did you get it? Why you?"

"Rachel gave it all to me. She came by looking for information. I work at the school now and when I heard she was Moony's sister and she showed me the letter Moony wrote,

I offered to help her find you."

"You work at the high school?"

"Yes. A long story. Music teacher."

"Why did you not tell me?"

"I didn't think you would come back for me. I offered to help Rachel, though."

"The satchel and stuff?" I asked with one eye on her and one eye on the prize sitting on the grass in front of me.

"The night Moony died, he tossed it into the trees, apparently to keep it safe. The police found it and gave it to his aunt. That's how Rachel got it. She came looking for you. She is smart. No doubt about that. I told her we were old friends, and if anyone could find you, it would be me."

"So, you read everything. Everything?"

"Yes. I probably shouldn't have, but I did." She studied me with probing eyes and a warm smile. She paused in between her words, almost in tune with some beat she could only hear. "I think it's all very wonderful, really. The stuff you wrote. It was very touching that someone could affect you so much."

"I don't know what to say. I honestly do not mind you read it. If anyone found it, I suppose . . ." I stopped my sentence trying to find the words and hoping maybe she didn't notice my incomplete thought.

"You suppose?"

"It never was meant for anyone to see. Moony read it, so he knew and now you. But I trust you."

"You trust me? Really? I owe you a box-load of albums and CDs I borrowed and you can still say you trust me; I'm pleasantly surprised."

"I always trusted you ever since that day."

She looked at me and could see my eyes staring into space, processing all that transpired. She reached out and grabbed my forearm. "I need to tell you something. Rachel tried to. She's the one who called me. She said you would be here."

"She called you tonight?"

"Yes. I asked her to. I was worried. She wanted to tell you everything, but you took off. I know what happened that night. I know what happened tonight. She called me on my cell, just after you left."

"I figured she did. Why else would any other adult be out here in the wee hours?"

"Fortunately, I was at the school, chaperoning the grad dance. Not too far really."

"So, what is it that Rachel needed to tell me?"

"It's about Laura. I tried to find her. After reading everything, I knew what I wanted to do, and told Rachel I would find her. We both knew it would be the only way to get you back."

"Good grief. You didn't have to do anything. I could handle it."

"Please just listen and remember we desperately tried."

"So you tried to find Laura?" I was almost saying it to myself, impressed by her deed.

"Yes, I did. It's why Rachel tried to speak to you. I knew you would come back. After all, I read, I know you. I've known you since we were six. I knew you would be back. I gave you a black eye and got you a detention and you still always were nice to me. I just knew. I'm so sorry."

"Sorry for what?"

"She moved away years ago. Someplace in Germany. I didn't contact her. We couldn't reach her." She let go of my arm, got up, and walked down the slight incline. She walked near the edge of the river and was gazing at the reflection of light on the water. I bit my lip and pushed off with both hands onto my feet. I walked slowly to her and stood next to her. Out of the corner of her eye, I could see a dot of soft blue looking at me. She then turned and analyzed my face, seeing me biting my lip. Her eyebrows raised in acknowledgment.

"Oh, my God! You know. You've known all along?" Her voice trembled at my revelation, her eyes wide.

"That she married years ago and moved? Yes, I've known that for a long time, to be honest. A very long time."

She gasped slightly almost in disbelief and partially in relief. "I don't understand. When I sent you the poem, if you knew you wouldn't find her, why?"

"Why did I come back?"

"Yes."

"I came back hoping to find myself again. What you sent me was a reminder that I left my soul back here when I retreated south. I needed to reclaim what was once mine. My soul."

"You're not mad at Rachel or me?"

"No. Especially now that I'll get all my music back." I could see her face give birth to a distinct smile. It was almost like she was suppressing it. She turned and walked back to where the satchel sat and picked it up and brought it back to me, her arms outstretched before me. "It's time it finally got back to its rightful owner."

I took it from her and slowly opened it. An old, beat-up notebook with pages and pages sticking out everywhere. I sighed in recognition of it. She finally broke the heavy silence as she saw my eyes glitter with moisture.

"I know it must hurt you. Everything. Moony. Not being able to tell Laura—and now her being so far away." Each word from her was melodic and soothing.

"I practiced, you know. Practiced all day that day what I was going to say."

"I have little doubt that you still recall every syllable." Her mood became playful suddenly.

"Yeah. I probably do."

Her eyes grew wide with the schoolgirl excitement of a new idea. "Why don't you tell me what you were going to say?"

"Oh, Janie. I would feel a bit awkward. It was so long ago."

"Awkward. You made me read that other poem you wrote for Laura. Remember. Christmastime."

"All along, you were on to me. I cannot believe it."

"You are so transparent to everyone but yourself. Now please tell me, don't be shy. I'll be completely honest."

"Maybe that's what I'm afraid of."

"I've done far worse to you. Now, please, for me." Her eyes waited for the words as if listening to them.

"Be mindful that I was only sixteen. It is a little amateurish." I didn't wait or expect an answer from her. I closed my eyes and rewound my mind. The words reappeared as if conjured by a sorcerer's spell.

"There's a saying that love sets on fire the one who finds it. At the same time, it seals his lips so that no smoke comes out. Well, I am nearly suffocated from the smoke now. You see, I obsessed with how I would feel. I now know with clarity and in peace that it was never about me. The love I feel gave my soul air to breathe. The way I see it is simple. From that first day, I knew I loved you, I have been fabric by fabric, thread by thread, knitting a coat to give you, made of the most enduring of all materials: my love. Like any great gift, I have no expectation of anything in return in this lifetime. All I hope for is you accept this gift. It is yours to store away if you wish for now. It will always be there for you to wear in this lifetime and beyond. I will find my happiness knowing it will keep you warm through eternity."

I stopped and opened my eyes. Janie stood smiling in front of me. "I assume you were going to give her your flight jacket that night as a symbol. Cool and sweet." She didn't wait for the affirmative nod. "Did you ever wonder what kind of reaction that would get?"

"To be honest, I was hoping for a smile back. That's what I told Moony, and I meant it."

"How about, I love you?" She grinned with her eyes flashing like a million fireflies. I may have been blinded by the light as my mind remained tangled in the past.

"That would have blown me away if Laura had responded anywhere close to that."

"Silly boy. It's not her saying it." She stood before me, eyes sparkling, and without me realizing it right away, she was holding both of my hands.

The realization flooded the chambers of my dry soul with fine mineral water. A million words danced in my mind. "Janie. I was not expecting." My voice trailed off and blended in with the water evaporating off the river.

"Of course, you weren't." She giggled with a hint of nervousness. Janie had always been confident and self-aware. I was now witnessing her vulnerability. I was overwhelmed with the complete trust she was showing me.

Suddenly the words tumbled from lips. "Are you sure? You read all this and . . . are you sure?"

She laughed at the childlike wonder I showed her. I was giving her an out, a way to take back the words. She could always repent for I would surely forgive her.

"I'm sure *because* I read all that. Sounds simple if you ask me."

"Crystal clear," I said, laughing.

"Understand that when I read what you wrote, it was such an intense flame that must have burnt inside you. It gets cold up here. The warmth of that fire attracted me because the source is so caring."

"I wrote this for someone else. I mean about someone else." I said it in a whisper.

"Of course, I know that. We've known each other since we were kids. I always liked you, but as I learned more about you, I liked you more. Knowing you had this in you and what you were capable of feeling, well, maybe you understand why I'm next to you today."

Her hand reached out and touched my cheek gently and slowly brushed it. Sparks erupted at my very depths, setting off fire upon fire. "Janie, I always considered you my friend. Not just any friend. A special one."

"Kiran, I know how much you loved her. Even over the years. I know you still do. Be honest."

A lie would have been easy, not for Janie. "Yes." My heart was content in the truth. "The love that awoke inside of me years ago was always part of me, the best part."

Janie continued my sentence. "And you always will. It will never change how I feel about you."

A gentle breeze swept over the river, and a quiet roar went up from the currents. My heart exploded in rhythm. "Follow me." I took Janie's hand in mine and with the other hand picked up the satchel. I led her to the edge of the river and kicked off my shoes and reached down and took off my socks. She followed my lead and took off her shoes and lifted up her skirt slightly. We waded a couple of feet into the water. I stopped and looked at her as I put the satchel down in the water and pushed it adrift into the river.

"I figure Moony needs something interesting to read."

"Are you sure? I know how much it means to you."

"I'm sure. It's only words. The feelings and emotions will exist beyond these words. Those words are for another time and another place. What is important to me now is here." I leaned over to her and held her by the wrist and kissed her on the lips. "If I let go, you're not going to slug me again, are you?"

"No. Only if you promise me one thing."

"I'm staying. For sure, I'm not leaving you."

Her face beamed, and before she spoke, I continued, "I

have no job right now and not many prospects. I may not be the best catch."

"I wouldn't worry about that. Follow me."

We walked back across the field and up and over the hill until we could see our old high school on the other side. The students had long since departed and there were faint lights that emanated from the school. I could see a memorial plaque at the entrance of the school and decided I needed to visit it with Marius and Rachel. I had already made my offering to the gods.

In the midst of our trek, she turned to me. "I've been teaching music here the last ten years. We could use a good English teacher."

"Janie, did you read my notebook? I can't teach English," I said, almost serious. "Unless proper spelling and grammar are optional."

"I will just say I know the principal very well. I don't think it'll be an issue." She smirked, pointing to the school parking lot.

There in the space reserved for the school principal, in bright black print on a white background were the words:

RESERVED FOR PRINCIPAL WOODSMITH

I looked at her in utter amazement. She unlocked the doors and led me into the school. We walked into my old English class. It was refurbished with a smart board, new desks, and chairs. I paused at the doorway and looked around the now empty room. My eyes looked at my old spot and darted across the room to the last seat at the back of the class at the far side. I stopped momentarily, beamed, and could almost feel a smile back. I then continued down the corridor.

She led me to the gym. Paper plates, cups, confetti, and ribbons were strewn everywhere. She maneuvered me to the middle of the dance floor. She took my hand and guided it partway to her hair.

"Go ahead. I know you've wanted to."

I reached out and caressed the blue ribbon dancing again at the back of her head and slowly untied it with both hands in her hair. My hands felt her soft blonde hair, and at that moment, I could feel her lips on mine. She slowly pulled her head back and began singing. I never knew how angelic her voice was.

She sang a song I recognized from my youth. One I had not heard in years. The lyrics danced off her tongue. I welcomed them all like an old lost friend seeking shelter from a storm.

She stopped waiting for me to answer, hoping to evoke a response.

"*I will dare,*" I replied.

She stopped with a whisper of a tear in her eye and a grin on her mouth as the wisps of ginger light slowly floated into the gym. We walked back to the corridor hand in hand. We found the nearest classroom and took a seat at the back of the class to watch the sky.

On the horizon, the sun slowly made its appearance in an explosion of orange.

"The moon will be gone soon," I whispered.

She looked at me. "When I started teaching as an assistant in an elementary school, one of the students asked me where the moon goes during the day. I told him that it's always there. You just can't see it because the sun's light is so bright.

"You know what he replied back? 'Ah, so it's like a dance they do together in the sky. Sometimes one takes the lead and sometimes the other.'"

I smiled and sat beside her while shivering ever so slightly. She rose, sliding behind me as she took off her shawl and draped it across my shoulders.

I felt warm.

Epilogue

Into my dreams, you flutter,
chasing the subtle moonlight.
Whispering to the air you touch,
Quiet, as the wind through an empty desert.
No longer does my living soul rest.
It sings and dances.
Until the envious light does come,
my soul hides and waits beneath
my vacant heart
and prays for the silent end of the day.
Back to sweet embrace is all I want,
when I will wade into blue seas
splashing visions onto these hollow walls.
Colors passionately entwine with each vibration
of this silent symphony.
Hope opens the window
for a humid soul,
dripping, wet and melting
with each vengeful dawn.
I sleep a little longer.
Stealing from time,
you nibble at my toes,
caress my palms
and kiss my open neck.
You bathe me in your shadow 'til
the jealous time cloaks the night in its damp towel,
presiding over this morning parade.

Beneath its orange aura merciless elephants
trample down the path toward my tender heart.
Hide from the eastern sun
and tuck the dream under my pillow!
The dreary and tired will soon awake.